> "There was, from the beginning,
> a palpable sense of something alien
> in the house."

So Gregory Craig began his second book on the supernatural. His first book on the occult had made him rich. He didn't know it could also make him dead.

GHOSTS
Ed McBain's most terrifying thriller

The 87th Precinct. Hard-nosed cops live with violent death every day. They are ready for any evil in this world. But can they face an evil from a world beyond? For even when the mind will not accept what the eyes see . . . the heart-stopping terror in their guts couldn't be more real.

Bantam Books by Ed McBain

CALYPSO
GHOSTS

GHOSTS
Ed McBain

BANTAM BOOKS
TORONTO · NEW YORK · LONDON

GHOSTS
*A Bantam Book | published by arrangement with
The Viking Press*

PRINTING HISTORY
*Viking edition published May 1980
A Selection of Literary and Mystery Guild May 1980
Bantam edition | May 1981*

This is for Ed Victor

1

They might have been ghosts themselves, the detectives who stood in the falling snow around the body of the woman on the sidewalk. Shrouded by the swirling flakes, standing in snow three inches deep underfoot, they huddled like uncertain specters against the gray façade of the apartment building behind the slain woman. The two Homicide men who stood on the pavement with Detective Cotton Hawes were wearing black overcoats and gray fedoras. Hawes was hatless. His red hair shrieked into the monochromatic hush, echoing the blood that stained the woman's clothing. There was a streak of white just above Hawes's left temple, the memento of a scuffle while investigating a burglary; it seemed almost a wider patch of the snow crystals that glistened in his hair.

The Homicide detectives stood with their hands in the pockets of their overcoats. This was four days before Christmas, and the time was 7:00 P.M. Monoghan had not yet bought a present for his wife; neither had Monroe. The stores would be open till nine tonight, and they had planned to go shopping the moment they were relieved at a quarter to eight. Instead, they'd taken the call from the Eight-Seven, and Christ alone knew how long they'd be here on the sidewalk with Hawes and his partner Carella, who was standing at the curb talking to the patrolman who'd been first at the scene.

"Musta been coming home with her groceries," Monoghan said.

"Yeah, look at that stuff all over the sidewalk," Monroe said.

"Wheaties," Monoghan said.

"She eats the breakfast of champions," Monroe said.

"*Used* to eat," Monoghan corrected.

"Knocked her ass over teacups," Monroe said.

"She's got good legs," Monoghan said.

The woman on the sidewalk seemed to be in her early thirties. She was a white woman, and she was wearing a plain cloth coat open over a white blouse, black skirt, and black boots. The front of the blouse, just under her left

1

breast, had been slashed when the knife entered her chest. The entire left side of the blouse was drenched with blood. The skirt had pulled back over her thighs when she fell to the sidewalk. She lay on her back, arms and legs akimbo, one fist clenched, the brown shopping bags scattered around her, one of them torn, their contents strewn. The strap of a black shoulder bag had fallen loose to her elbow.

"Did you check her handbag yet?" Monoghan asked.

"I'm waiting for the techs to get here," Hawes said.

"Guy who did it could be in Outer Mongolia, time the techs get here."

"They're on the way," Hawes said.

"Did you call the M.E.?"

"I'm not new on the job," Hawes said.

"Oh, he's not new on the job," Monoghan said to his partner.

"He's *old* on the job," Monroe said, and took out his handkerchief and blew his nose. He was coming down with a cold, and he didn't need to be standing here in the snow with a smartass dick from the Eighty-seventh. But in the city for which these men worked, the appearance of Homicide detectives at the scene of a murder was mandatory; the detectives who'd answered the squeal at the precinct would be handling the case and were required to file regular reports with Homicide.

Detective Steve Carella turned from the radio motor patrol car. He was a tall, slender man with the casual stride of an athlete, and he came walking over slowly, seemingly lost in thought, his head bent. His eyes—squinted now against the falling snow—were somewhat slanted, giving his face a faintly Oriental look that intensified the semblance of deep, inscrutable meditation. Like Hawes, he was hatless. Like Hawes, he was wearing a plaid mackinaw over a woolen shirt and corduroy trousers; they had just returned from a fruitless warehouse stakeout when the call came in.

"Beat officer recognizes the woman," he said. "She lives in the building right here; he doesn't know her name."

"I told your partner here to go through her bag," Monoghan said.

"New regs call for the techs to do that," Carella said.

"Fuck the new regs," Monoghan said. "We're standin' here freezin' our asses off, and you're worried about the new regs."

"You want to authorize it?" Carella said.

"I ain't *authorized* to authorize it," Monoghan said.

2

"Okay then, we wait for the techs. Meanwhile, I'd like to talk to the security guard. You want to listen in?"

"Better than standing out here in the snow," Monoghan said.

"I'll start the sketch, Steve," Hawes said.

"Better get them Crime Scene signs up," Monroe advised over his shoulder, and followed Carella and Monoghan into the building. The apartment complex was part of a citywide project to reclaim deteriorating slums. It rose in concrete and glass splendor on the outer fringes of the Eighty-seventh, replacing half a dozen tenements that had previously squatted here. The security guard was a white man in his early sixties, Carella guessed, wearing a gray uniform with a yellow and blue Security Patrol patch on the left arm. He looked apprehensive and wary, as if the cops were about to blame him for something.

"I'm Detective Carella, Eighty-seventh Squad," Carella said. "These men are from Homicide."

The security guard nodded and then wet his lips.

"What's your name?" Carella asked.

"Jimmy Karlson."

"Are you the regular security guard here, Mr. Karlson?"

"Yes, sir. Well, there are four of us—five, actually, if you count the one after midnight."

"What are your shifts?"

"Six A.M. to twelve noon, noon to six P.M., six to midnight, and midnight to six. Four shifts. On the midnight to six, we've got an extra man patrolling the grounds with a dog."

"What time did you come on tonight, Mr. Karlson?"

"Six. Well, actually a little after. I don't have snow tires on the car, and I got held up by the storm."

"Do you know we've got a dead lady outside?" Monoghan asked.

"Yes, sir, I do. The man who found her came in here to make the call, in fact."

"Who was that?" Carella asked.

"I don't know. He said there was somebody hurt on the sidewalk and asked if he could use the phone. Soon as he made the call, he walked off. I guess he didn't want to get involved."

"And what did *you* do?" Monroe asked.

"I went outside to see what it was."

"Did you recognize the woman?"

"Yes, she lives here in the building. Esposito, Apartment Seven-oh-one."

3

"What's her first name?" Monoghan asked.

"I don't know."

"She married, single?" Monroe said.

"Married. Her husband should be home any minute, in fact."

"Did you see anything that happened out there?" Carella asked.

"No, sir, I did not. The security desk is sort of off to the right here. I couldn't have seen anything happening out there on the sidewalk."

"Did you see Mrs. Esposito when she left the building?"

"No, sir, I did not. That would have been this morning sometime. She goes to work, you see, and she usually gets home just after I've come on—maybe ten after, a quarter after six."

"Stopped to pick up some groceries, just like I told you," Monoghan said to Monroe.

The patrolman Carella had been talking to just a few minutes earlier came walking over from the r.m.p. car. He looked troubled. He hesitated before opening the glass door to the lobby, and then stamped snow from his shoes, and again hesitated before he said what he had to say, like a king's messenger fearful of losing his head for bringing bad news.

"We got another one," he said. "Upstairs in Apartment Three-oh-four."

The second call had come into Communications Division at exactly ten minutes past seven. The dispatcher had put the information into his computer, and the two-hour sector scan of previously reported incidents had confused him at first. Car Adam Eleven had been dispatched to the same scene a half hour earlier: a cutting on Jackson and Eighth. But the first victim had been reported as a white female bleeding on the sidewalk outside 781 Jackson, and this new call was from a hysterical woman in Apartment 304, and she was telling the police there was a man stabbed on the bedroom floor up there, and could they please send somebody right away? The dispatcher had radioed Adam Eleven again and told him to check upstairs, and the patrolman who took the call in the r.m.p. car said, "You got to be kidding," and then walked over to where the detectives were talking with the security guard.

The woman who'd called the police was waiting in the third-floor corridor for them. She was a white woman in her

4

early twenties, Carella guessed, with brown eyes and black hair, and she so closely resembled his wife that he hesitated mid-stride as he came out of the elevator and then did a double take and realized this could not be Teddy; Teddy was home in Riverhead with Fanny and the kids. The resemblance was not lost on Hawes. He glanced swiftly to Carella and then looked down the corridor again to where the woman stood just outside the open door to Apartment 304. She was wearing her overcoat, the shoulders still damp with melted snow. There was a look of utter panic on her face and in her eyes. The cops came down the corridor in a flying wedge, Carella and Hawes in the forefront, Monoghan and Monroe behind them. Monroe was thinking this was just what they needed, another stiff.

"Where is he?" Carella asked.

"Inside," the woman answered. "In the . . . the bedroom."

The front door opened into a foyer with a mirror and mail table facing the entrance. The apartment branched off on both sides of the hall. On the right, Carella could see through an open door into the kitchen. On the left was the living room. They came through quickly, no signs of disorder, the room decorated neatly and expensively in clean modern, several paintings on the walls, a bar unit with a whiskey decanter and two glasses on it, both of them sparkling, everything neat and clean and orderly. The bedroom was quite another matter. From the moment they walked through the door, they knew this was going to be a bad one.

The room was in complete disarray. The drawers of the white Formica dresser had been pulled out, the clothing thrown all over the floor. Men's clothes and women's clothes, undershorts and brassieres, lingerie and pajamas, dress shirts and silk blouses, baby doll nightgowns and socks, crew-neck sweaters and bikini panties lay strewn in androgynous confusion on the thick pile rug. The doors on both closets were open, and the clothes had been pulled from their hangers and scattered over the floor, the bed, and the chairs. Men's sports jackets and suits, women's gowns and skirts, high-heeled pumps, walking shoes, loafers, topcoats, trenchcoats, overcoats—all twisted a tortuous trail across the rug to where the dead man lay on the side of the bed farthest from the door.

He was a white man—in his early fifties, Carella guessed—wearing blue slacks, a lime green T-shirt, and a dark blue cardigan sweater. No shoes. His hands were bound behind his back with a twisted wire hanger. The T-shirt had been slashed to ribbons. There were stab wounds on his chest and his throat and his hands and his arms. One ear dangled loose from the right side of his head, where it had been partially severed. Carella looked down at the dead man and felt again a familiar mixture of horror and sadness—the same each and every time—a revulsion for the violence that had reduced a human being to a fleshly pile of bloody rubble, a grief for the utter wastefulness of it. He turned to Hawes and said, "If the M.E.'s downstairs, we'd better get him up here."

"Better get another team of techs, too," Monoghan said. "Otherwise, we'll be here all night."

On one wall of the room, facing the windows that overlooked the River Harb, there was a long white Formica desk with a typewriter on it. A ream of yellow paper rested on the desk top, just beside an ashtray brimming with cigarette butts. A sheet of paper was in the typewriter. Without touching either the paper or the machine, Carella leaned over the desk and read the typewritten words:

There was, from the beginning, a palpable sense of something alien in the house. I had been called here to investigate the claim that poltergeists had invaded the premises, and there was no question now, before I had taken three steps into the entrance hall, that the claim was valid. The air virtually hummed with unseen specters. When there are ghosts in a place

"Suicide note?" Monroe asked behind him.

"Sure," Carella said. "The guy's laying on the floor with his

6

hands tied behind him and thirty-six knife wounds in his chest ..."

"How do you know there's thirty-six?" Monoghan said.

"Make it forty," Carella said. "It's obviously a suicide."

"He's pulling our leg," Monroe said.

"He's joshing us."

"He's a very humorous cop."

"All the cops at the Eight-Seven are very humorous."

"You want to know something, Carella?"

"Go fuck yourself, Carella."

The woman who looked like Carella's wife was waiting in the living room outside. She had not yet taken off her coat. She sat in one of the stark white easy chairs, her hands clasped over the bag in her lap. As they talked, Hawes came back with the Medical Examiner and led him silently into the bedroom. The second team of lab technicians arrived, and they went about their task like a hush of pallbearers.

"When did you find him?" Carella asked.

"Just before I called the police."

"Where'd you make the call?"

"Here. Right here." She indicated the white telephone resting on the bar unit alongside the decanter and the two clean glasses.

"Touch anything else in the apartment?"

"No."

"Just the phone."

"Yes. Well, the doorknob, when I came in. I unlocked the door, and then I called to Greg, and when I got no answer, I went straight to ... to the bedroom and ... and ... that was when I saw him."

"And then you called the police."

"Yes. And ... and I went outside to ... to wait for you. I didn't want to wait in here. Not with ... not with ..."

Carella took out his notebook and busied himself with finding a clean page. He suspected she was about to cry, and he never knew what to do when they began crying.

"Can you tell me his name, please?" he asked gently.

"Gregory Craig," she said, and paused, and looked into Carella's eyes, and he felt she expected some sort of response she wasn't getting. Puzzled, he waited for her to say something more. "Gregory Craig," she repeated.

"Would you spell that for me, please?"

"G-R-E-G-O-R-Y."

"And the last name?"

"C-R-A-I-G."

"And your name?"

"Hillary Scott." She paused. "We weren't married."

"Where were you coming from, Miss Scott?"

"Work."

"Do you usually get home at about this time?"

"I was a little late tonight. We were waiting for a call from the Coast."

"What sort of work do you do?"

"I work for the Parapsychological Society." She paused and then said, "I'm a medium."

"A medium?"

"Yes."

"I'm sorry, what . . . ?"

"I'm gifted with psychic powers," she said.

Carella looked at her. She seemed sane enough, sitting there in her wet overcoat, her hands clenched on her pocketbook, her eyes beginning to mist with tears. In his notebook, he wrote the word "Medium" and then put a question mark after it. When he looked up again, she was dabbing at her eyes with a handkerchief she'd taken from her bag.

"Where did Mr. Craig work?" he asked.

"Here," she said.

"Here?"

"He's a writer," she said, and paused. "Gregory Craig, the writer."

The name meant nothing to Carella. In his notebook, under the word "Medium," he wrote "Victim writer," and then realized she had said, "Gregory Craig, *the* writer," and further realized she'd been expecting recognition of the name all along. Cautiously he asked, "What sort of writing did he do?"

"He wrote *Deadly Shades*," she said, and again looked directly into his eyes, and he was certain this time that he was supposed to recognize the title of the book Craig had written —if it *was* a book. He did not ask what it was.

"And he worked here in the apartment, is that it?" he said.

"Yes, in the bedroom. There's a desk in the bedroom. That's where he worked."

"All day long?"

"He usually began about noon and quit about six."

"And wrote, uh, books or—what is it he wrote, actually, Miss Scott?"

8

"You haven't read *Deadly Shades?*"

"No, I'm sorry."

"It's already sold three million copies in paperback. The movie is being shot right this minute."

"I'm sorry, I'm not familiar with it."

She said nothing. She simply looked at him. He cleared his throat, glanced at his notebook again, looked up, and said, "Any idea who might have done this?"

"No."

"Did Mr. Craig have any enemies that you might know of?"

"None."

"Had he received any threatening telephone calls or letters in the past—"

"No."

"—several weeks? Anything like that?"

"No, nothing."

"Did he owe anybody money?"

"No."

"How long have you been living in this building, Miss Scott?"

"Six months."

"Any trouble with the neighbors?"

"None."

"When you got home tonight, was the door locked?"

"Yes. I told you I opened it with my key."

"You're sure it was locked?"

"Yes."

"You heard the tumblers falling when you turned your key?"

"Yes, I know it was locked."

"Did anyone beside you and Mr. Craig have a key to this apartment?"

"No," she said. "Just the two of us."

"Thank you, Miss Scott," he said, and closed the notebook. He tried a smile and then said, "I'll have to look for *Deadly Shades.* What's it about?"

"Ghosts," she said.

The head security officer was waiting downstairs with Karlson when Carella got back to the lobby. His name was Randy Judd, and he was a big, beefy Irishman in his sixties. He told Carella at once that he used to be a patrolman working out of the Three-Two. He also mentioned there'd never been any trouble here at Harborview since the complex was built a year ago. Not even a burglary. Nothing.

"The security is very tight here at Harborview," he said.

"Very tight," Karlson said. He still looked apprehensive, as if more than ever certain the cops would somehow blame him for this.

"Mr. Karlson," Carella said, "you told me a little while ago that you came to work at six tonight . . ."

"A little after."

"A little after six, right. Did you announce anyone to Mr. Craig between the time you came on and . . ."

"No, sir, I did not."

"Is that usual procedure? Announcing visitors?"

"Standard practice," Judd said.

"*All* visitors," Karlson said. "Even delivery boys."

"Then what happens?"

"When we get clearance from the tenant, the visitor can go up."

"On the elevators there?"

"Unless it's a delivery. The service elevator is around to the back."

"And no one came here asking for Mr. Craig?"

"No one."

"Who had the shift before you? The noon to six?"

"Jerry Mandel."

"Have you got his home phone number?" Carella asked.

"Yes, but it won't do you any good," Judd said.

"Why not?"

"He was going skiing this weekend," Karlson said. "Had his skis on top of the car, in fact, was driving upstate the minute I relieved him."

"When will he be back?"

"Day after Christmas," Judd said. "He had vacation time coming. I gave him the okay. He's a big skier."

"Do you know where he went?"

"Someplace upstate," Karlson said.

"Did he mention the name of the hotel or the lodge?"

"No, he didn't."

"Can I have that phone number anyway?" Carella said.

"Sure," Judd said. "It's right in the office here."

From the office phone Carella dialed Mandel's home number. He let the phone ring twelve times and then hung up.

"No luck, huh?" Judd said.

"No," Carella said, and shook his head.

10

"I told you," Karlson said. "He was leaving straight from here."

"Any way of getting in this building except through the front entrance?" Carella asked.

"The garbage is collected out back," Judd said. "There's a big door there; we unlock it when the garbage truck gets here."

"What kind of lock on it?"

"Schlage dead bolt."

"Who has the key?"

"Building superintendent."

"Is he here now?"

"Sure. You want to talk to him?"

The building superintendent was a black man named Charles Whittier. He was eating his dinner when Judd introduced him to Carella. A television set was going in the other room, and Carella could see through the open door to where a black woman in robe and slippers was sitting watching the screen, a dinner plate on her lap. She got up the moment she realized visitors were in the apartment and closed the door. Behind the closed door the television voices droned. A cop show. Carella hated cop shows.

"Mr. Whittier," Carella said, "a murder was committed upstairs in Apartment Three-oh-four, we clocked the call in at seven-ten. Was the door back here open at any time today?"

"Yes, sir, it was," Whittier said.

"Who opened it?"

"I did."

"When?"

"Twelve noon, when the garbage truck come."

"Did you let anyone inside the building?"

"Just the garbage men. We keeps the garbage cans inside here cause we don't want rats to get at them. There's rats in this neighborhood, you know."

"*Every* neighborhood," Judd said, defending his turf.

"So the garbage men come inside here to pick up the cans, is that it?"

"They're not obliged to," Judd said, "but we give them a few bucks each year around this time."

"How many garbage men?" Carella asked.

"Two," Whittier said.

"Were you here while they were in the building?"

"Yes, sir."

11

"Either of them remain inside the building?"

"No, sir. They picked up the garbage, and I locked the door after them."

"Did you open that door again at any time after that?"

"Yes, sir, I did."

"When?"

"When it started snowing bad. I wanted to get out and do a little shoveling before it got too heavy to move."

"What'd you shovel?"

"The ramp back there. So's the garbage truck can get in tomorrow."

"Did you lock the door while you were outside?"

"No, sir, I did not. But I could see it all the time I was shoveling."

"See anybody come in here?"

"No, sir."

"Were you watching the door every minute?"

"No, sir, not every minute. But I had my eye on it."

"What time was this?"

"When I started shoveling? Musta been about five-thirty thereabouts."

"And you didn't see anyone going into the building?"

"No, sir. I'da called Security right off had I seen anybody."

"Okay, thanks, Mr. Whittier," Carella said. "Sorry to have interrupted your meal."

On the way upstairs, Judd said, "Security's very tight here at Harborview, like I told you."

Carella was thinking it hadn't been tight enough to prevent a murder on the third floor or one outside on the sidewalk.

2

There were nineteen wounds on the body of Gregory Craig. Carella received the typewritten list from the morgue at Buena Vista Hospital ten minutes before Hawes came in with the morning newspaper. The list read:

WOUNDS CHART, GREGORY CRAIG:

1. Slash wound across throat 1¾" long.

2. Slash wound across throat just under first one, 2½" long.

3. Stab wound 1½" right of midline just over collarbone.

4. Stab wound 4½" right of midline and 4" above nipple.

5. Stab wound over midline and in line with nipples.

6. Slash wound on chest beginning on midline approx. 5" below chin and tailing downward and to the left 2" long.

7. Stab wound 1½" left of midline and over collarbone.

8. Stab wound 8½" left of midline and 3" below nipple.

9. Stab wound (entry and exit) midway between elbow and armpit, on inside of arm.

10. Slash wound 1" long on outside of left wrist.

11. Slash wound 1¼" long on inside of right wrist.

12. Stab wound on back 15" below base of skull and 5½" left of midline.

13. Stab wound on back 15" below base of skull and 3" left of midline.

14. Stab wound on back 13¼" below base of skull and 3½" left of midline.

15. Stab wound on back 12" below base of skull and 8" left of midline.

16. Stab wound on back 20" below base of skull and 3½" left of midline.

17. Slash wound on inside of ring finger of right hand.

18. Stab wound (entry and exit) on top side of middle finger of right hand.

19. Slash wound right side of head above ear and tailing downward 1½" long.

That was a whole hell of a lot of stab and slash wounds. They didn't quite add up to the estimate Carella had given the Homicide cops at the scene, but they were sufficient to indicate that whoever had killed Craig had really and truly wanted him dead; you do not hack away at a person nineteen times unless you want to make sure. On the other hand, Marian Esposito—as she'd been identified from a driver's license in her shoulder bag—had been stabbed only once, just below the left breast, the blade entering her chest and her heart and apparently killing her at once. If the crimes were related, as they seemed to be, the logical assumption was that she had got in the killer's way as he was fleeing the scene of the first murder. Even before Hawes came in with the morning paper, Carella had decided that the line of investigation should concentrate on Craig. He marked the case folder R-76532," and on the folder for Marian Esposito, he wrote in the words "Companion Case R-76532" following *her* case number, R-76533.

The squadroom that Friday morning, December 22, was

relatively quiet. The suicides would not start till Christmas Eve, and then they'd taper off a bit till New Year's Eve, when there'd be another rash of them. Miscolo in the Clerical Office had casually mentioned that there'd be a full moon on New Year's Eve. The full moon would compound the number of suicides. Holidays and full moons, it never failed. In the meantime, there'd been an increase in incidents of shoplifting and picking pockets, but burglaries, muggings, rapes, and robberies had fallen off; go figure it. Maybe all the burglars, muggers, rapists, and armed robbers were out shopping the department stores and getting their pockets picked.

The squad's duty chart hung on the wall alongside the water cooler, where the lieutenant figured it was certain to be read. The Police Department respected no holidays, but the duty chart for every Christmas Eve and Christmas Day normally listed almost exclusively the names of Jewish detectives who had traded off with their Christian colleagues. This year, however, things were different. How was this year different from all other years? This year, Christmas and the first day of Chanukah happened to fall on the very same day—December the twenty-fifth, naturally—providing ample evidence of the brotherhood of man and the solidarity of the democratic ideal. It caused problems only for the cops. Everybody wanted to be off on Monday, when the twin holiday occurred. But everybody *couldn't* be off on Monday because then all those cheap thieves out there would run amok.

Compromise.

In police work, as in marriage, compromise was essential. Henny Youngman's repertoire included a joke about the man who wants to buy a new car and his wife who wants to buy a mink coat. They compromise. The wife buys a mink coat and keeps it in the garage. Steve Carella and Meyer Meyer compromised by tossing a coin. Carella won. He would work on Christmas Eve, and Meyer would work on the first day of Chanukah. But that was before the Eight-Seven caught the double homicide. With a homicide case, you worked it into the ground during those first few important days. Carella had the gnawing suspicion that he'd be with this one a long time—hot pastrami sandwiches and a bottle of soda pop in the squadroom on Christmas Day. Terrific.

At his desk across the room, alongside one of the wire-mesh grilles that protected the squadron from missiles flung at the windows by an unappreciative precinct citizenry—and incidentally kept any prisoners from leaping out to the street

15

below—Detective Richard Genero sat typing up a report on a burglary that was three weeks old. Genero was a short dark man with curly black hair and brown eyes. He had recently taken to wearing Benjamin Franklin eyeglasses whenever he typed his reports, presumably to better his spelling. He still spelled "perpetrator" as "perpatrater," a fatal failing in any police department. He had a transistor radio going on his desk, and the strains of "Silent Night, Holy Night" flooded the squadroom. Carella listened to the music and guessed that if Lieutenant Byrnes walked in this very minute, Genero would be back walking a beat before the new year. Genero typed in time to the music. Carella wondered when he would ask how to spell "surveillance."

It was 10:37 A.M. by the squadroom clock. The snow of the night before had ended shortly before dawn, and the sky outside was now a blue as bright as a bride's garter. From beyond the squadroom windows, Carella could hear the sounds of tire chains jangling, an appropriate accompaniment for "Jingle Bells," which now replaced "Silent Night" on Genero's transistor. He did not much feel like working today. He had told the twins he'd take them to see Santa Claus sometime this week—but that, too, was before the double homicide.

"Where is everybody?" Hawes said from beyond the slatted wooden railing that divided the squadroom from the corridor outside. "Did you see this, Steve?" he asked, and came through the gate in the railing. "We got ourselves a biggie." He tossed the morning paper onto Carella's desk and then went to the water cooler. The paper was folded open to the page opposite the book review.

The obit on Gregory Craig told Carella that the man had written a best-selling book titled *Deadly Shades*, which presumably had been based on his own experiences with ghosts in a house he'd rented in Massachusetts three summers ago. The book had topped the nonfiction best-seller list for a full year and had been reprinted six months ago, garnering a paperback advance of $1.5 million. The motion picture was currently being filmed in Wales, of all places, with a British star playing Craig and a galaxy of fading well-known actresses in cameo roles as the shades who'd plagued his hoped-for vacation. The obit went on to say that he'd written a half dozen novels before turning out his nonfiction blockbuster, listing them all by title and quoting some of the reviews the newspaper had given him over the past twelve years. There'd been a hiatus of five years between his last

16

novel and the ghost book. His sole survivor was listed as Miss Abigail Craig, a daughter. The obit did not mention the murder of Marian Esposito, Companion Case R-76533.

"What do you think?" Hawes said, and crumpled the paper cup he was holding, and tossed it at Carella's wastebasket, missing.

"I think they saved us some legwork," Carella said, and opened the Isola telephone directory.

When Abigail Craig opened the door for them at eleven-twenty that morning, she was wearing an expensively tailored suit over a silk blouse with a scarf tied at the throat, brown high-heeled boots, gold hoop earrings. They had called first to ask if they might come over, and she had seemed a bit reluctant on the phone, but they chalked this off to the natural grief and confusion that normally followed the death of an immediate member of the family. Now, sitting opposite her in a living room dominated by a huge and lavishly decorated Christmas tree, they weren't sure whether she was at *all* grieved or confused. She seemed, in fact, more interested in getting to her hairdresser than in telling them anything about her father. Her hair looked fine to Hawes. *All* of her looked fine to Hawes.

She was one of those creamy blondes with a flawless complexion usually attributed to British women who ride horses. Her eyes were a brilliant green fringed with lashes as blond as her hair; her face was somewhat narrow, with high cheekbones and a generous mouth that looked richly appointed even without lipstick. Her upper lip flared a bit, showing perfect white teeth even when she wasn't speaking. Hawes loved the ones with an overbite. Hawes wished they were here to exchange Christmas gifts instead of to ask questions about a dead man who seemed to hold little or no interest for the cool beauty who sat opposite him in brown high-heeled boots, her legs crossed.

"I'm sorry I have to rush you," she said, "but my appointment is at noon, and Antoine is clear across town."

"*We're* sorry to break in like this," Hawes said, and smiled. Carella looked at him. They hadn't *broken* in at all. They had called a half hour ago and carefully prepared her for their visit.

"Miss Craig," Carella said, "when did you last see your father ailve?"

"A year ago," she said, startling him.

"And not since?"

17

"Not since."

"How come?"

"How *come?*" Abigail said, and arched one eyebrow. "I'm not sure I know what you mean." Her voice was Vassar or Bryn Mawr out of Rosemary Hall or Westover: Her manner was irritated and impatient. Carella had never felt comfortable with these long, cool, poised types, and she was doing little now to ease his distress. He looked at her for a moment and debated his approach. He decided to lay it on the line.

"I *mean,*" he said, "isn't that a bit unusual? An only daughter . . ."

"He has another daughter," she said flatly.

"Another daughter? I was under the impression . . ."

"More or less," Abigail said. "She's *young* enough to be his daughter anyway."

"Who's that?" Carella asked.

"Hillary."

"Do you mean Hillary Scott?"

"Yes."

"I see."

"Do you?" Abigail said, and reached for a cigarette in an enameled box on the endtable. Lighting it, she said, "Let me put it to you simply," and blew out a stream of smoke, and then put the gold lighter back on the table. "Ever since the divorce my father and I haven't got along. When he took up with the Spook, that was the end. Period. Finis. Curtain."

"By the Spook . . ."

"Hillary."

"And when did he . . . take up with her, Miss Craig?"

"Shortly after *Shades* was published—when—*all* the creeps in the universe were coming out of the woodwork with ghosts of their own."

"You're referring to *Deadly Shades?*"

"My father's big moneymaking masterpiece," Abigail said, and crushed out the cigarette.

"It was published when?"

"The hardcover edition? A year and a half ago."

"And he met Hillary Scott shortly after that?"

"I don't know *when* he met her. I didn't find out about them until Thanksgiving a year ago. God knows how long they'd been living together by then. Invited me over for the big turkey dinner. 'Hello, darling,'" she said, mimicking broadly, " 'I'd like you to meet Hillary Scott, my lady friend.' His *lady* friend!" she said, her eyes flashing. "Fucking little twenty-two-year-old spook hunter."

18

Carella blinked. He was used to all sorts of language in the squadroom and on the streets; you couldn't be a cop for as long as he'd been one and still expect people to say "darn" and "shucks." But the obscenity had sounded completely out of place in this festively decorated living room on Hall Avenue. Hawes, on the other hand, was watching Abigail with an intensity bordering on instant obsession; he loved the ones who said "fuck" through their overbites.

"So, uh, the last time you saw your father," Carella said, "was . . ."

"Thanksgiving last year. When he introduced me to the Spook. That was it. The last straw."

"What were the *other* straws?"

"The divorce was the big thing."

"And when was that?"

"Seven years ago. Right after *Knights and Knaves* was published."

"That's one of his novels, isn't it?"

"His *best* novel. And his *last* one." She took another cigarette from the enameled box, held the lighter to it, and blew out a stream of smoke in Hawes's direction. "The critics savaged it. So naturally, he took it out on Mother. Decided that Stephanie Craig, poor soul, was somehow to blame for what the critics had said about his book. Never once realized that the book was truly a marvelous one. Oh, no. Figured if the *critics* said it was awful, why then, it *had* to be awful. And blamed Mother. Blamed her for the life-style—one of his favorite words—that had caused him to write his universally panned novel. Said he wanted out." Abigail shrugged. "Said he needed to 'rediscover' himself—another favorite Gregory Craig utterance." She dragged on the cigarette again. "So he *rediscovered* himself with a piece of crap like *Shades*."

"Is your mother still alive?" Hawes asked.

"No."

"When did she die?"

"Three summers ago."

"How?"

"She drowned. They said it was an accident."

"They?"

"The Coroner's Office in Hampstead, Massachusetts."

"Massachusetts," Carella said.

"Yes. She drowned in the Bight, two miles from where my father was renting his famous haunted house."

"This was how many years after the divorce?"

"Four."

19

"And they spent their summer vacations in the same town?"

"She never got over it," Abigail said. "She wanted to be near him. Whenever he went . . ." She shook her head.

"A minute ago, Miss Craig, you said the Coroner's Office . . ."

"Yes."

"Do *you* believe your mother's death was accidental?"

"She was on the swimming team at Holman U when she was a student there," Abigail said flatly. "She won three gold medals."

The report from the Mobile Crime Lab was waiting on Carella's desk when they got back to the squadroom. It stated that the lock on the door to the Craig apartment was a Weiser dead bolt, meaning that it could be unlocked on both sides—inside and out—only with a key. There had been no key in the lock on the inside of the door. There were no jimmy marks on the jamb, no scratches on the perimeter of the lock or around the keyway, no signs of forced entry. The apartment's service entrance—opening into the kitchen from a small alcove lined with garbage cans—was similarly equipped with a Weiser dead bolt. Again, there were no signs of forced entry. A check of the lock on the big door leading to the rear ramp of the building showed no signs of forced entry. Whoever had killed Gregory Craig was a person who either lived in the building and was known to the security guard on duty or was someone known to Craig himself. If the killer had first been announced by the security guard who was off skiing his brains out someplace, then Craig had given the okay to send him upstairs. There were sixty apartments in the Harborview complex. Carella made a note to begin a door-to-door canvass of the tenants, and he made a further note to ask Byrnes for additional manpower on the case—fat chance of getting it three days before Christmas.

At twelve-twenty that afternoon he called the Craig apartment, hoping to catch Hillary Scott there. He let the phone ring an even dozen times, replaced the cradle on its receiver, looked up the number for the Parapsychological Society in Isola, and dialed it.

"I've been trying to reach you," Hillary said.

"What about, Miss Scott?"

"Didn't you get my message?"

"No. I'm sorry, I just got back."

"I gave my message to somebody up there. Somebody with an Italian name like yours."

Carella looked across the room to where Genero was eating a sandwich at his desk, munching in time to "Deck the Halls."

"I'm sorry, what were you calling about?" he said.

"The autopsy. I understand they want to do an autopsy."

"That's right, an autopsy is mandatory in any trauma case."

"Absolutely *not*," she said.

"Miss Scott, I'm afraid this isn't something . . ."

"What happens when Greg's essence passes over?" Hillary said. "If you cut him open and take out his insides, what happens when he gets to the spirit world?"

"I have no control over this," Carella said. "An autopsy is mand—"

"Yes, I heard you. Who *do* I talk to?"

"About what?"

"About stopping the autopsy."

"Miss Scott, the Medical Examiner's Office has probably already begun work on the body. It's vital that we establish the cause of death so that when the case comes to trial . . ."

"It's vital that Greg's spirit pass over intact!"

"I'm sorry."

There was a silence on the line.

"I've heard about too many mutilated spirits," Hillary said.

"I'm sorry," he said again. "Miss Scott, the reason I was calling . . ."

"Far too many," she said, and again there was a silence on the line. Carella waited. There was no sense continuing the argument. The autopsy would be performed whatever Hillary Scott said or did. As he'd just told her, the M.E.'s Office had probably already begun work. At the morgue, the body of Gregory Craig would be slit open like a slab of beef, the vital organs removed and tested, the skull lifted back on a tab of flesh to expose the brain. When the corpse was later displayed in a funeral home, none of the mourners would realize they were looking at the hollow shell of what had once been a man. The silence lengthened. Carella assumed he had made his case.

"I was wondering if you could meet us at the apartment later today," he said.

"What for?"

"There's the possibility that Mr. Craig may have been surprised by a burglar. We want to know if anything's missing, Miss Scott, and the only way we can determine that is with someone who knows what *should* be in the apartment."

"It wasn't a burglar who killed Greg," Hillary said.

"Why do you say that?"

"It was a ghost."

Sure, Carella thought. A ghost tied Craig's hands behind him with a wire coat hanger. A ghost stabbed him nineteen times in the chest, the back, the arms, the throat, the hands, and the head with a *ghost* knife the lab boys had not been able to find anywhere in the apartment. The same ghost knife that had most likely been used on Marian Esposito, Companion Case R-76533.

"I felt a very strong flux in that apartment yesterday," Hillary said.

"Can you meet us there in an hour?" Carella asked.

"Yes, certainly," she said. "But it wasn't a burglar."

If it hadn't been a burglar, it had certainly been someone who'd helped himself—or herself—to a great many things in the Craig apartment. According to Hillary Scott, there had been some $300 in the bill compartment of Craig's wallet when she'd left the apartment yesterday morning at ten. She knew because she'd asked him for cab fare to the office, and he'd fanned out a sheaf of fifties, searching for smaller bills. The money was gone now, but Craig's credit cards—seven of them in all—hadn't been touched. His jewelry box, open on the dresser top, had been looted of a gold Patek Philippe wristwatch with a gold band, a pair of gold Schlumberger cuff links set with diamonds, a gold pinkie ring with a lapis stone, and a gold link bracelet. Hillary was uncertain about the value of Craig's missing jewelry, except for the gold bracelet, which she'd brought for him herself last Christmas and which had cost $685. She suspected the Patek Philippe wristwatch had cost somewhere in the vicinity of $6,500. She was more specific about the jewelry that was missing from the box she kept in the top drawer on her side of the dresser. All of it had been given to her by Gregory Craig during the year and a half they'd been living together. She listed the stolen items as:

One Angela Cummings hand-carved root bracelet of Burmese jade and eighteen-karat gold at $3,975.

One Elsa Peretti snake hairband of eighteen-karat gold at $510.

One eighteen-karat gold choker set with diamonds at $16,500.

One pear-shaped diamond pendant set in platinum with an eighteen-inch chain of eighteen-karat gold at $3,500.

One emerald-cut diamond set in a platinum ring at $34,500.

One pair of eighteen-karat gold earrings with mabe pearls at $595.

One pair of diamond earrings set in platinum at $1,500.

One rope choker of eighteen-karat yellow and white gold at $2,950.

One bracelet of eighteen-karat pink, yellow, and white gold at $1,250.

And two fourteen-karat gold bangle bracelets at $575 each.

In addition to the jewelry stolen from the box, she told them she was missing from the dresser drawer itself an Elsa Peretti bean-shaped bag of twenty-four-karat gold lacquered with magnolia wood at $2,500 and a Chopard bracelet-watch of eighteen-karat gold set with diamonds at $14,500. She had kept the watch in the original case it had come in; the case was still in the drawer, a black velvet exterior, a white satin lining—but the watch was gone. She knew the value of the jewelry Craig had given her because they had recently made an insurance appraisal on all of it.

"But not on *his* jewelry?" Carella asked.

"Yes, his, too. But we had to get separate policies because we aren't married. I was only familiar with what mine came to."

"And what was that, offhand?" Hawes asked.

"Offhand, it was exactly eighty-three thousand four hundred and thirty dollars."

"That's a lot of stuff to have kept loose in a dresser drawer," Carella said.

"Greg was planning on buying a wall safe," Hillary said. "Anyway, it was all insured. And besides, the security here is very good. We wouldn't have taken the apartment if we weren't promised such tight security."

"Anything else missing?" Hawes said.

"Was he wearing his college ring?" Hillary asked.

"There was no jewelry on the body."

"Then that's missing, too."

"What college?" Carella asked.

"Holman University. Where he met his former wife."

"What kind of ring?"

"Gold with an amethyst stone."

"Where did he wear it?"

"On the ring finger of his right hand."

Carella remembered the Wounds Chart: *Slash wound on inside of ring finger of right hand.* Had the killer used the knife to pry the ring loose from Craig's finger? Had he come into the apartment armed, or had he used a knife he'd found on the premises? If he'd come here specifically to commit a burglary, then how had he got through the "tight" security downstairs? Would Craig have admitted a stranger to the apartment, someone who'd later stolen in excess of $83,000 worth of jewelry and killed him before leaving? But Hillary Scott insisted it was not a burglar.

"The flux is strongest in this room," she said. She walked to the desk facing the windows and put her hands on its surface. "He was here at the desk."

"He?"

"A male spirit," she said, running her hands lightly over the desk top. "Young. Black hair and brown eyes." Her own eyes were closed; her hands flitted lightly over the surface of the desk; she swayed as she spoke. "Searching for something. Seeking. Restless. A restless spirit."

Carella looked at Hawes. Hawes returned the look. Carella was wondering how somebody who so closely resembled his wife could be so certifiably nuts. Hawes was wondering what she'd be like in the sack—would she go into a trance from all the flux? And then he felt immediately incestuous because the damn girl looked so much like Teddy Carella. He turned away from Carella's gaze, as though fearful his mind had been read.

"Anything missing from the desk?" Carella asked.

"May I open it?" she said. "Are your people through with it?"

"Go ahead," Carella said.

She opened the drawer over the kneehole. A tray full of paper clips, rubber bands, and pencils. A staple remover. A box of key tags. A box of loose-leaf reinforcers. She closed that drawer and opened the file drawer to the right of the kneehole. It contained a sheaf of index folders lettered with names.

"Is that Craig's handwriting?" Carella asked.

24

"Yes, shhhhh."

"What are those names?"

"Ghosts," she said, "shhhhhh," and passed her hands lightly over the folders. "He was searching here."

"If he was," Hawes said, "the lab boys'll have prints."

"Spirits do not leave fingerprints," she said, and Carella thought, *Nutty as a fruitcake.*

"Those names . . ."

"Yes, ghosts," she said. "Cases he planned to investigate for authenticity. Ever since he wrote *Shades,* he's received calls and letters from all over the world, people reporting ghosts."

"Anything missing that you can tell?" Hawes asked.

"No, but he was in here. I know he was in here."

She closed the file drawer and opened the drawer above it. A ream of yellow manila paper, nothing else. "Here, too," she said. "Searching, seeking."

"Did Mr. Craig ever keep anything of value in this desk?" Carella asked.

"His files are extremely valuable," Hillary said, and abruptly opened her eyes.

"Maybe he *was* looking for something," Hawes said. "Everything thrown around the room the way it was."

"Yes, positively," Hillary said.

"And *found* it," Carella said.

Hillary looked at him.

"More than eighty-three thousand dollars' worth of jewelry."

"No, it wasn't that. It was something else. I don't know what," she said, and passed her hands over the air as though trying to touch something the detectives could not see.

"Let's check the kitchen," Carella said. "I want you to tell us if any knives are missing."

They checked the kitchen. On a magnetic wall rack, over the counter top, there were seven knives of varying sizes, one of them a ten-inch-long chef's knife. According to Hillary, all the knives were there. They opened the cabinet drawers. She counted the table cutlery and the assortment of slicing and paring knives in the tray and told them nothing was missing.

"Then he came here with it," Carella said.

Hillary closed her eyes again, and again spread her fingers wide, and pressed her palms against the empty air. "Looking for something," she said. *"Something."*

It was Cotton Hawes who caught the flak from Warren Esposito. The flak was perhaps well deserved; Hawes might have encountered the same indignation in any major city of the world, Peking and Moscow not excluded. Whatever the politics of a nation, the fact remained that if you knocked off somebody in the public eye, *that* murder was going to get more attention from the police than the murder of a wino or a scaly-legs hooker. Marian Esposito was neither a drunk nor a prostitute; she was, in fact, the secretary for a firm that specialized in selling gift items via direct mail. But there was no doubting the fact that she was somewhat less important than Gregory Craig, the best-selling writer. As her husband, Warren, paced the squadroom floor and raged at him, Hawes wondered whether they'd have given *her* case the same attention they were giving Craig's had *she* been the one found with nineteen knife wounds in her and *he'd* been the one lying outside the building with a single stab would. He decided the priorities would have been the same. Craig was "important"; Marian Esposito was only another corpse in a city that grew corpses like mushrooms.

"So what the hell *are* you doing?" Esposito shouted. He was a tall, hulking man with thick black hair and penetrating brown eyes. He was dressed on this Friday afternoon in blue jeans and a turtleneck sweater, a fleece-lined car coat open and flapping as he paced the floor. "There hasn't even been a single cop to *see* me, for Christ's sake! I had to make six phone calls before I discovered where they'd taken her! Is that what happens in this city? A woman is stabbed to death in front of her own apartment building and the police sweep her under the rug as if she never existed?"

"There's a companion case," Hawes said lamely.

"I don't give a damn about your companion case!" Esposito shouted. "I want to know what you're doing to find my wife's murderer."

"It's our guess . . ."

"Guess?" Esposito said. "Is that what you're doing up here? Guessing?"

"It's our opinion . . ."

"Oh, now it's an opinion."

"Mr. Esposito," Hawes said, "we think the person who killed Gregory Craig only accidentally killed your wife. We think he may have been . . ."

"Accidentally? Is it an accident when somebody sticks a knife in a woman's heart? Jesus *Christ!*"

26

"Perhaps that was an unfortunate choice of words," Hawes said.

"Yes, perhaps," Esposito said icily. "My wife is dead. Somebody killed her. You have no real reason to believe it was the same person who killed that writer on the third floor. No real reason at all. But he's a *celebrity*, right? So you're concentrating all your efforts on him, and meanwhile, whoever killed Marian is running around loose someplace out there," he said, and whirled and pointed toward the windows, and then swung around to face Hawes again, "and I can't even find out where her body is so I can make funeral arrangements."

"She's at the Buena Vista Morgue," Hawes said. "They're finished with the autopsy. You can . . ."

"Yes, I *know* where she is. I know *now*, after six phone calls and a runaround from everybody in the Police Department. Who do you have answering your phones up here? Mongolian idiots? The first two times I called no one had even *heard* of my wife! Marian Esposito, sir? Who's that, sir? Are you calling to report a crime, sir? You'd think somebody's goddamn *bicycle* was stolen, instead of . . ."

"Most calls to the police are handled downtown at Communications," Hawes said. "I can understand your anger, Mr. Esposito, but you can't really expect a dispatcher, who handles hundreds of calls every hour, to know the intimate details of . . ."

"Okay, who *does* know the intimate details?" Esposito said. "Do *you* know them? They told me downstairs that you're the detective handling my wife's case. So, all right, what are you . . . ?"

"My partner and I, yes," Hawes said.

"So what the hell *are* you doing?" Esposito said. "She was killed yesterday. Have you got any leads; do you even know where to *start*?"

"We start the same way each time," Hawes said. "We start the way you yourself would start, Mr. Esposito. We have a corpse—in this case, *two* corpses—and we don't know who made it a corpse, and we try to find out. It's not like in the movies or on television. We don't ask trick questions, and we don't get sudden flashes of insight. We do the legwork, we track down everything we've got, however unimportant it may seem, and we try to find out *why*. Not *who*, Mr. Esposito, we're not in the whodunit business here. There are no mysteries in police work. There are only crimes and the

27

person or persons who committed those crimes. With an armed robbery, we know the *why* even before we answer the telephone. With a murder, if we can find out why, we can often find out who—if we get lucky. We've got three hundred unsolved murders in the Open File right this minute. Next year we may crack a half dozen of them—*if* we get lucky. If not the murderer will stay loose out there someplace"—and here he pointed to the windows, as Esposito had done earlier—"and we'll *never* get him. Murder is a one-shot crime except where the killer is a lunatic or a criminal who kills in the commission of another felony. Your average murderer kills once, and never again. Either we catch him and put him away, and he never gets the *chance* to kill again, or else he folds his tent and disappears."

Esposito was staring at him.

"I'm sorry," Hawes said. "I didn't mean to make a speech. We're aware of your wife, Mr. Esposito; we are very *much* aware of her. But we feel the primary murder was the one in Apartment Three-oh-four, and that's where we're starting. When we get Gregory Craig's murderer, we'll also have the person who killed your wife. That's what we feel."

"What if you're wrong?" Esposito said. His anger was gone; he stood there with his hands in the pockets of the fleece-lined coat and searched Hawes's face for some reassurance.

"If we're wrong, we'll start all over again. From the beginning," Hawes said, and hoped to Christ they were not wrong.

The call from Jerry Mandel, the schussing security guard, came just as Carella and Hawes were getting ready to go home. They had by then had a fruitless meeting with Lieutenant Byrnes, who told them he positively could not double-team his men at Christmastime and advised that they conduct the door-to-door canvass of Harborview all by their lonesomes even if it took till St. Swithin's Day, whenever *that* was. He informed them, besides, that he had received a call from the attorney of one Warren Esposito, who claimed the murder of Gregory Craig was receiving preferential consideration over the murder of his client's wife, and if some people didn't start shaking their asses, they'd be hearing from a friend of the lawyer, who only just happened to work downtown in the district attorney's office. Byrnes reminded them that in this fair city murder was perhaps the one great equalizer and that regardless of race, religion, gender, or occupation, one corpse

28

was to be treated exactly as the next corpse—an admonition both Carella and Hawes accepted with a bit of salt.

They had next received the autopsy reports on both Gregory Craig and Marian Esposito, but those learned medical treatises told them hardly anything they did not already know. They would have turned in their shields at once had they not at least suspected that the respective causes of death were multiple stab wounds in the case of Gregory Craig and a single stab wound in the case of Marian Esposito. The medical examiners were not paid to make guesses—not anywhere in the linked reports was there the slightest speculation that the same instrument might have been used in both murders. The reports *did* tell them that Gregory Craig had been drinking before his murder; the alcoholic concentration in the brain was 16 percent, and the milligrams of ethyl alcohol per milliliter of blood were 2.3. The brain analysis indicated that Craig had reached that stage of comparative intoxication in which "less sense of care" had been the physiologic effect. The blood analysis indicated that he had been "definitely intoxicated." They made a note to check with the Spook—they had already begun calling her that—about whether Craig habitually drank while he worked. Carella remembered the two clean glasses alongside the decanter in the living room and wondered now whether the killer had washed them after the murder. The list of articles found in the bedroom did not include either a whiskey bottle or a glass.

The call from Jerry Mandel came at 6:20 P.M. Carella was just taking his .38 Chiefs Special from the file drawer of his desk, preparatory to clipping it to his belt, when the phone rang. He snatched the receiver from its cradle and glanced up at the clock. He had been working the case since eight this morning, and there was nothing more he could do on it today, unless he felt like rapping on the sixty doors in Harborview, which he did not feel like doing till morning.

"Eighty-seventh Squad, Carella," he said.

"May I please speak to the detective handling the murders at Harborview?" the voice said.

"I'm the detective," Carella said.

"This is Jerry Mandel. I heard on the radio up here . . ."

"Yes, Mr. Mandel," Carella said at once.

"Yes, that Mr. Craig was killed, so I called the building to find out what happened. I talked to Jimmy Karlson on the six to midnight, and he said you people were trying to locate me. So here I am."

"Good, I'm glad you called, Mr. Mandel. Were you working the noon to six yesterday?"

"I was."

"Did anyone come to the building asking for Mr. Craig?"

"Yes, someone did."

"Who, would you remember?"

"A man named Daniel Corbett."

"When was this?"

"About five o'clock. It was just starting to snow."

"Did you announce him to Mr. Craig?"

"I did."

"And what did Mr. Craig say?"

"He said, 'Send him right up.' "

"Did he *go* up?"

"Yes, he did."

"You saw him go up?"

"I saw him go into the elevator, yes."

"At about five o'clock?"

"Around then."

"Did you see him come down again?"

"No, I did not."

"You quit at six . . ."

"At about a quarter after, when Jimmy relieved me. Jimmy Karlson."

"And this man—Daniel Corbett—did *not* come down while you were on duty, is that right?"

"No, sir, he did not."

"Can you tell me what he looked like?"

"Yes, he was a youngish man, I'd say in his late twenties or early thirties, and he had black hair and brown eyes."

"What was he wearing?"

"A dark overcoat, brown or black, I really don't remember. And dark pants. I couldn't see whether he was wearing a suit or a sports jacket under the coat. He had a yellow scarf around his neck. And he was carrying a dispatch case."

"Was he wearing a hat?"

"No hat."

"Gloves?"

"I don't remember."

"Would you know how he spelled his name?"

"I didn't ask him. He said Daniel Corbett, and that was the name I gave Mr. Craig on the phone."

"And Mr. Craig said, 'Send him right up,' is that correct?"

"Those were his exact words."

30

"Where are you if I need you?" Carella asked.

"The Three Oaks Lodge, Mount Semanee."

"Thank you, you've been very helpful."

"I liked Mr. Craig a lot," Mandel said, and hung up.

Carella put the receiver back on the cradle, turned to Hawes with a grin, and said, "We're getting lucky, Cotton."

Their luck ran out almost at once.

There were no Daniel Corbetts listed in any of the city's five telephone directories. On the off chance that Hillary Scott might have known him, they called her at the apartment and were not surprised when the phone was not answered there; not many people chose to remain overnight in an apartment where a murder had been committed. They called her office and spoke to a woman there who said everybody had gone home and she was just the cleaning woman. They searched the Isola directory for a possible second listing for Hillary Scott. There was none. They ran down the list of sixty-four Scotts in the book, hoping one of them might be related to the Spook. None of the people they called had the faintest idea who Hillary Scott might be.

It would have to wait till morning after all.

3

Hillary Scott called Carella at home at eight-thirty Saturday morning. He was still in bed. He propped himself up on one elbow and lifted the receiver of the phone on the night table.

"Detective Carella" he said.

"Were you trying to reach me?"

"Yes," he said.

"I sensed it," Hillary said. "What is it?"

"How'd you get my home phone number?" he asked.

"From the phone book."

Thank God, he thought. If she'd plucked his home phone number out of thin air, he'd begin believing all *sorts* of things. There was, in fact, something eerie about talking to her on the telephone, visualizing her as she spoke, conjuring the near-duplicate image of his wife, who lay beside him with her arms wrapped around the pillow, her black hair spread against the pillowcase. Teddy Carella was a deaf-mute; she had not heard the ringing telephone; she did not now hear Carella's conversation with the woman who looked so much like her. He wondered, abruptly, whether—if Teddy had a voice—it would sound like Hillary Scott's.

"You tried me at the apartment, didn't you?" she said.

"Yes."

"I'm here now," she said. "I came back to get some clothes. The flux was strongest around the telephone."

"Yes, well, good," he said. "Can you tell me where you're staying now, so in case I need to . . . ?"

"You can reach me at my sister's," she said. "Her name is Denise Scott; the number there is Gardner 4–7706. You'd better write it down; it's unlisted."

He had already written it down. "And the address?" he said.

"Thirty-one-seventeen Laster Drive. What did you want, Detective Carella?"

"The security guard who normally has the noon to six at Harborview called last night. Jerry . . ."

"Jerry Mandel, yes."

"Yes. He said Mr. Craig had a visitor at five P.M. on the day he was murdered. A man named Daniel Corbett. Does that name mean anything to you?"

There was a silence on the line.

"Miss Scott?"

"Yes. Daniel Corbett was Greg's editor on *Shades.*"

"He was described to me as a young man with black hair and brown eyes."

"Yes."

"Miss Scott, when we were in the apartment yesterday . . ."

"Yes, I know what you're about to say. The spirit I described."

"A young male, you said. Black hair and brown eyes." Carella paused. "Did you have any reason for . . . ?"

"The flux was strongest at the desk."

"Aside from the flux."

"Only the flux," she said.

"But you do know Daniel Corbett."

"Yes, I know him."

"Is he, in *fact,* a young man?"

"Thirty-two."

"With black hair and brown eyes?"

"Yes."

"Where do I reach him, Miss Scott?"

"At Harlow House."

"Where's that?"

"That's the name of the publishing firm. Harlow House. It's on Jefferson and Lloyd."

"Today's Saturday. Would you know his home number?"

"I'm sure Greg has it in his book."

"Are you in the bedroom now?"

"No, I'm in the living room."

"Could you go into the bedroom, please, and look up the number for me?"

"Yes, of course. But it wasn't Daniel I was sensing yesterday. It wasn't Daniel at all."

"Even so . . ."

"Yes, just a minute, please."

He waited. Beside him, Teddy rolled over, and stirred, and then sat up and blinked into the room. She was wearing a cream-colored baby doll nightgown he'd given her for her birthday. She stretched, and smiled at him, and then kissed him on the cheek, got swiftly out of bed, and padded across the room to the bathroom. No panties. The twin crescents of her buttocks peeped from below the lace hem of the short gown. He watched her as she crossed the room, forgetting for a moment that she was his own wife.

"Hello?" Hillary said.

"Yes, I'm here."

The bathroom door closed. He turned his full attention back to the medium on the telephone.

"I've got two numbers for him," Hillary said. "One in Isola, and the other up in Gracelands, upstate. He has a place up there he goes to on weekends."

"Let me have both numbers, please." In the bathroom, he heard the toilet flushing and then the water tap running. He wrote down the numbers and then said, "Thank you, Miss Scott, I'll be in touch."

"It wasn't Daniel," she said, and hung up.

Teddy came out of the bathroom. Her hair was sleep-tousled, her face was pale without makeup, but her dark eyes were sparking and clear, and he watched her as she crossed to the bed and for perhaps the thousandth time thanked the phenomenal luck that had brought her into his life more years ago than he cared to remember. She was not the young girl he'd known then, she did not at her age possess the lithe body of a twenty-two-year-old like Hillary Scott, but her breasts were still firm, her legs long and supple, and she watched her weight like a hawk. Cozily she lay down beside him as he dialed the first of the numbers Hillary had given him. Her hand went under the blanket.

"Hello?" a man's voice said.

"Mr. Corbett?"

"Yes?" The voice sounded a trifle annoyed. Carella realized it was still only a little before nine on a Saturday morning—the big Christmas weekend no less. Under the blanket, Teddy's hand roamed familiarly.

"I'm sorry to bother you so early in the morning," Carella said. "This is Detective Carella of the Eighty-seventh Squad. I'm investigating the murder of Gregory Craig."

"Oh. Yes," Corbett said.

"I was wondering if I might stop by there a little later this morning," Carella said. "There are some questions I'd like to ask you."

"Yes, certainly."

Carella looked at the bedside clock. "Would ten o'clock be all right?"

Beside him, Teddy read his lips and shook her head.

"Or eleven," Carella corrected, "whichever is more convenient for you."

"Eleven would be better," Corbett said.

"May I have the address there, please?"

Corbett gave it to him. As Carella wrote, Teddy's hand became more insistent.

"I'll see you at eleven," he said, "thanks a lot," and hung up, and turned to her.

"I have to call Cotton first," he said.

She rolled her eyes heavenward.

"It'll only take a minute."

She released him as suddenly as she had grasped him and with a sigh lay back against the pillow, her hands behind her head, the bedclothes lowered to her thighs, the baby doll gown carelessly exposing the black triangular patch of hair below the hem.

"Cotton," he said, "I've made an appointment with Daniel Corbett for eleven o'clock. He's down in the Quarter. Can you meet me there?"

"How'd you find him?" Hawes asked.

"The Spook called."

"Out of the blue?"

"Flux. Write this down, will you?" Carella said, and read off the address. "Eleven o'clock."

"See you there," Hawes said, and hung up.

Carella put the receiver back on the cradle and rolled over to Teddy. Her hands were still behind her head; there was an expression of utter boredom on her face.

"Okay," he said.

She sat up suddenly. Her hands fluttered on the air. He watched her fingers, reading the words they formed, and then began grinning.

"What do you *mean,* you've got a headache?" he said.

Her hands moved again, fluidly, fluently.

I always get headaches when people stay on the phone too long, she said.

"I'm off the phone now," he said.

She shrugged airily.

"So what do you say?"

She shrugged again.

"You want to fool around a little?" he asked, grinning.

Her eyes narrowed smokily, in imitation of some bygone silent-movie star. She wet her lips with her tongue. She lowered one strap of the gown from her shoulder, exposing her breast. Her hands moved again. *I want to fool around a lot, big boy,* she said, and licked her lips again, and fell greedily into his arms.

The Quarter on that Saturday before Christmas was thronged with last-minute shoppers, who milled along the sidewalks and swarmed into the stores in search of bargains they would never find. There was a time, not too many decades ago, when this section of the city was still known as the *Artists'* Quarter, and when it was possible to find here first-rate paintings or pieces of sculpture, hand-fashioned silver and gold jewelry, leather goods the equal of any tooled in Florence, lavish art books and prints, blouses and smocks hand-stitched in Mexico, wood carvings and jade, pottery and exotic plants—all at reasonable prices. Them days was gone forever, Gertie. No longer was it possible to rent a garret here and starve in it. No longer was it possible to find anything of quality at less than exorbitant prices. The name had changed those many years ago, and the area's uniqueness had vanished with it; the Quarter was now only another tourist attraction in a city that laid its traps like a fur trader. And still the shoppers came, ever hopeful of finding something here they could not find in the fancy shops lining Hall Avenue uptown.

As everywhere else in the city, the lampposts were now entwined with yuletide ropes and garlands of pine or holly. The storefront windows were sprayed with clouds of white paint in a vain attempt to simulate frost. Behind the plate glass, beds of cotton sprinkled with blue sequins were intended to evoke memories of snow-covered meadows. The huge Christmas trees in the area's still-existing plazas and squares were festooned with outdoor bulbs that glowed feebly in the late-morning gloom. The sky had turned cloudy once again, and the plowed snow in the gutters was now the city's favorite color: grime gray. The pavements had been shoveled only partially clear of the earlier snowfall, and there were treacherous icy patches to navigate. Nothing deterred the avid late shoppers. They plunged ahead like salmon swimming upstream to mate in icy waters.

Daniel Corbett lived in one of the area's remaining mews. A sculpted black wrought-iron fence enclosed a small courtyard paved with slate and led to the hidden front door of a house in an alleyway protected from the side street by a stand of Australian pines. The door was painted bright orange, and there was a massive brass knocker on it. Had the door been anywhere near the sidewalk, the knocker would have been stolen in ten minutes flat. As it was, Carella decided Corbett was taking an enormous risk leaving it hanging out there in

burnished invitation. He lifted the heavy brass and let it fall.
Once, twice, again. Hawes looked at him.

"He knows we're coming, doesn't ... ?"

The door opened.

Daniel Corbett was a young and handsome man with
straight black hair and brown eyes, an aquiline nose out of
The History of the Decline and Fall of the Roman Empire, a
mouth out of *The Razor's Edge*, and a jaw out of *Brighton
Rock*. He was, in addition, wearing a red smoking jacket with
a black velvet collar, straight out of *Great Expectations*. He
was altogether a literary man.

"Mr. Corbett?" Carella said.

"Yes?"

"Detectives Carella and Hawes," he said, and showed his
shield.

"Yes, come in, please," Corbett said.

What Corbett had promised in the flesh was now fully
realized in the shell. The wood-paneled entrance foyer opened
into a library lined with bookshelves that supported the
weight of an entire publishing house's output for the past ten
years or more. Jacketed books in every color of the spectrum
added a festive holiday note to the rich walnut paneling.
Books bound in luxuriant leather provided a proper touch of
permanence. A fire blazed on the hearth, flames dancing in
yellows, reds, and blues undoubtedly generated by a chemi-
cally impregnated log. A Christmas tree stood in one corner
of the room, decorated with delicate hand-blown German
ornaments and miniature tree lights manufactured in Hong
Kong. Corbett walked to where he had left a pipe burning in
an ashtray beside a red leather armchair. He picked up the
pipe, puffed on it, and said, "Please sit down." Carella looked
around for Dr. Watson but couldn't see him anywhere in
evidence. He sat in one of the two upholstered chairs facing
the red leather chair. He felt like ringing for his nog. He
wanted to take off his shoes and put on his velvet slippers. He
wanted to cook a Christmas goose. He wanted to be looking
forward to Boxing Day, whatever *that* was. Hawes sat in the
chair beside him. Corbett, as befitted his station as master of
the domicile, sat in the red leather chair and puffed on his
pipe.

"So," he said.

"So," Carella said. "Mr. Corbett, I'll come straight to the
point. On Thursday afternoon, at about five o'clock—some
two hours before Mr. Craig's body was found—a man named

Daniel Corbett arrived at Harborview and announced himself to the . . ."

"What?" Corbett said, and almost dropped his pipe.

"Yes, announced himself to the security guard in the lobby. The guard phoned upstairs, and Mr. Craig told him to send Corbett right up. Corbett was described—"

"Daniel Corbett?"

"—was described as a young man with black hair and brown eyes."

"Incredible," Corbett said.

"Mmm," Carella said. "So where were you Thursday afternoon at five o'clock?"

"At the office," Corbett said.

"Harlow House?"

"Harlow House."

"Anybody there with you?"

"Only the entire staff. We were having our annual Christmas party."

"What time did the party start, Mr. Corbett?" Hawes asked.

"Three o'clock."

"And ended when?"

"At about seven-thirty."

"Were you there the entire time?"

"I was."

"With anyone in particular or just the entire staff?"

"I spent some time with people who can vouch for my presence."

"Who were those people?" Carella asked. "Can you give us their names?"

"Well . . . *one* person in particular."

"Who?"

"One of our juvenile book editors, a woman named Priscilla Lambeth."

"Were you with her at five o'clock?"

"Yes, I guess it was five o'clock."

"And you say she'll corroborate that?"

"Well . . . I'm not sure she will."

"Why not?"

"She's married, you see."

"So?"

"So she may not be willing to admit having been in a . . . somewhat compromising position."

"How compromising was the position?" Hawes asked.

38

"I was fucking her on the couch in her office," Corbett said.

"Oh," Hawes said.

"At five o'clock?" Carella said.

"At five o'clock and again at six o'clock."

"Do you know her home number?"

"You surely don't intend *calling* her?" Corbett said.

"We can visit her instead."

"Really, gentlemen . . ."

"Mr. Corbett, one of your authors was killed last Thursday, and a man fitting your description and giving your name was reportedly at the scene of the crime two hours before the body was found. That's serious, Mr. Corbett. We don't want to break up any happy marriages, but unless Mrs. Lambeth can confirm that you were with *her* at five o'clock, instead of riding the elevator up to Craig's apartment . . ."

"Her number is Higley 7–8021."

"Okay to use your phone?"

"Yes, certainly," Corbett said, and indicated a phone resting on one corner of the bookshelf. Carella lifted the receiver, dialed the number Corbett had just given him, and waited. Corbett was watching him intently; his face had gone pale. A woman answered the phone on the fifth ring.

"Hello?" she said. Her voice was tiny and barely audible, as suited an editor of juvenile books.

"Mrs. Lambeth?" Carella said.

"Yes?"

"This is Detective Carella, I'm investigating the murder of Gregory Craig. I wonder if I may talk to you privately for a few moments. Are you alone?"

"Yes, I am."

"We're here with Daniel Corbett . . ."

"Oh."

"A colleague of yours . . ."

"Oh."

"And he tells us you can vouch for his whereabouts at five o'clock Thursday afternoon."

"Oh."

"Can you?"

"I . . . suppose so," she said, and hesitated. "Where did *he* say he was?"

"Where do *you* say he was, Mrs. Lambeth?"

"In my office, I guess."

"Was he or wasn't he?"

39

"Yes, I suppose he was."

"At five o'clock?"

"Well ... at about four-thirty, I guess it was. It's difficult to remember exactly."

"You went to your office together at four-thirty, is that it?"

"About four-thirty, yes."

"How long did you stay there?"

"Until about six-thirty. Is that what *he* told you?"

"Yes, that's what he told us."

"About the editorial meeting in my office?"

"Uh-huh," Carella said.

"Well, fine," she said, and sounded suddenly relieved. "Is that all?"

"For now, yes."

"Oh." She hesitated. "Does that mean you'll be calling again?"

"Maybe."

"I'd appreciate it if you called at the office next time," she said. "My husband doesn't like me bringing business into the home."

I'll bet, Carella thought, but said nothing.

"The number there is Carrier 2–8100. Extension forty-two."

"Thank you," Carella said.

"Please don't call here again," she said, and hung up.

"Okay?" Corbett said.

"Yeah," Carella said. "Who do you suppose was up there at Harborview using your name?"

"I have no idea."

"Is it common knowledge that you're Craig's editor?"

"In the trade, I suppose."

"How about outside the trade?"

"I don't think many people outside the trade would know it."

"Have any magazine or newspaper articles mentioned you as his editor?"

"Well, yes, come to think of it. There was a story on Greg in *People* magazine. It mentioned me, and it also ran a picture of us together."

"Then it's entirely possible that someone *outside* the trade . . ."

"Yes, I suppose so."

"How long have you known Priscilla Lambeth?" Hawes asked suddenly.

"Not long."

"How long?"

"She's new with the company."

"How new?"

"She joined Harlow House in the fall."

"Have you been intimate with her since then?"

"What business is that of yours?" Corbett said, suddenly climbing onto his high horse.

"We have only her word for where you were at five o'clock Thursday, Mr. Corbett. If this is a long-standing affair . . ."

"It isn't."

"Thursday was the first time, huh?" Hawes said.

"I find this embarrassing," Corbett said.

"So do I," Hawes said. *"Was* it the first time?"

"No."

"You've been with her before?"

"Yes."

"How often?"

"It started last month," Corbett said, and sighed.

"How often have you seen her since then?"

"Two or three times."

"That's all?"

"Yes. This isn't anything *serious,* if that's what you're suggesting. Pris has no reason to alibi me. Nor do I *need* an alibi. I was nowhere near Greg's apartment on Thursday. I was exactly where I told you I was, in Pris's office, on Pris's couch."

"Wasn't that a bit risky?"

"Nothing's risky at a Christmas party."

"So this is just a casual little fling, right?" Hawes said.

"If that's how you wish to put it."

"How do *you* wish to put it, Mr. Corbett?"

"It's casual, yes."

"How was your relationship with Craig?" Carella asked.

"Professional."

"Meaning what?"

"Meaning he sent me a book, and I liked it and recommended a buy. I worked on it with him, and Harlow published it."

"When was this?"

"We published it a year and a half ago. It was on our summer list."

"When did the book come in?"

"About ten months before that."

"Through an agent?"

41

"He has no agent. It came in addressed to an editor who was no longer with us. I recognized the name at once, of course; I'd read a couple of his novels in college."

"But this was nonfiction."

"Yes. A change of pace. Quite unlike anything he'd ever done before. I fell in love with it at once."

"When you say you worked on it with him . . ."

"It didn't require very much editing. Memory lapses—blue eyes on page twelve, green eyes on page thirty—some minor cutting here and there, but for the most part it was clean. I wish *all* my books were that clean."

"And that was the extent of your relationship?"

"No, he was working on another book when . . . when he was killed. We'd had correspondence about it, and many, many phone calls. He was having a difficult time."

"How about personal meetings?"

"Lunches, yes."

"When was the last time?"

"Oh, two weeks ago, I would imagine."

"Did he mention he was having difficulty with the new book?"

"Yes, that was why we met."

"What did you advise him?"

"What *can* an editor advise? He'd had a dry spell before, between his last novel and *Shades*. I told him this one would pass, too."

"Did he believe you?"

"He seemed to believe me."

"Mr. Corbett," Carella said, "there was a sheet of paper in Craig's typewriter, and it seemed to me—I'm not an editor, I don't know about such things—but it seemed like the *beginning* of a book. The opening paragraph, in fact."

"I don't think so, no," Corbett said, shaking his head.

"I don't remember it exactly, but I'm sure he wrote something about coming into a house for the first time . . ."

"Oh, yes. But you see, Greg was compiling a dossier of individual cases. About supposedly true supernatural happenings."

"Supposedly true?"

"Well . . . you know," Corbett said, and smiled. "What you saw in his typewriter may have been the beginning of just one *chapter* in the book."

"How long had he been working on it?"

"For the past year or so."

"How many chapters did he have?"

"Four."

"In a year?"

"I told you he was having difficulty. He kept rewriting it over and over again. It simply wasn't coming the way he wanted it to. *Shades* was a difficult act to follow, believe me. Greg wasn't as familiar with the nonfiction form as he was with novels. Not as sure of his ground, do you know what I mean? Not even sure *Shades* wasn't a fluke."

"Did he tell you that?"

"He didn't have to. The man was a quivering mass of insecurity."

"Did he mention anything else that was troubling him?"

"Nothing."

"No threatening letters or telephone calls?"

"Nothing."

"Crank calls?"

"Every author on the face of the earth gets crank calls."

"Did he mention any?"

"Not specifically, no. But I know he had his telephone number changed last month, so I'm assuming that was the case."

"Okay, thanks," Carella said. "Mr. Corbett, we may want to get in touch with you again, so . . ."

"Don't leave town, huh?" Corbett said, and smiled. "I used to edit mysteries on my first job in publishing."

"I wasn't about to say that," Carella said.

"What were you about to say?"

"I was about to say . . ." Carella hesitated. "That's what I was about to say," he said.

In the street outside, as they walked to where Carella had parked the car, Hawes said, "You weren't *really* about to say that, were you?"

"Yeah, I was."

"Don't leave *town?*"

"Words to that effect."

It was beginning to snow again. When they reached the car, Carella unlocked the door on the curb side and then went around to the driver's side. Hawes leaned over to pull up the lock-release button. Carella got in behind the wheel, shoved up the visor with its hand-lettered CITY DETECTIVE ON DUTY sign, and then started the car. They sat waiting for the heater to throw some warmth into it.

"What do you think?" Hawes asked.

"I think we'll have to check further with some of the other people at Harlow. I don't like having only her word for where he was, do you?"

"No, but on the other hand, she's a married woman who was getting laid in her own office, so it's not likely she was lying, is it?"

"Unless this is something more than the casual fling he *says* it is, in which case she could have been lying to protect him."

"Maybe," Hawes said. "But I'll tell you, Steve, it sounded casual to me."

"How so?"

"If it isn't casual, you don't say you were *fucking* somebody. You say you were making love, or you were alone together, or you were intimate, or whatever. But you don't say you were fucking somebody on her couch. That's casual, Steve. Take it from me, that's casual."

"Okay, it's casual."

"And besides, if he went up there to kill Craig, why would he announce himself to the security guard? Why didn't he say he was somebody from *Time* or *Newsweek* or *Saturday Review?* Why give his own name?"

"So Craig would let him in."

"And so the security guard would remember it later on? No way."

"Maybe he *didn't* go up there with the specific purpose of killing him. Maybe they got into an argument . . ."

"The killer brought the knife with him," Hawes said.

"Yeah," Carella said.

"So?"

"So what the hell do I know?" Carella said, and wiped at the misting windshield with his gloved hand. He was thoughtful for a moment. The wipers snicked at the sticking snowflakes. "All right," he said, "here's what I think. I think we ought to call Jerry Mandel up there in Mount Semanee and get him back to the city right away. I want to run a lineup on Daniel Corbett. Meanwhile, since we're so close to the courthouses down here, I think we ought to try for an order to toss his apartment. More than eighty-three thousand bucks' worth of jewelry was stolen from Craig's place, and that isn't the kind of stuff you can get rid of in a minute, especially if you're an editor and not familiar with fences. What do you say?"

"I say I'm hungry," Hawes said.

They stopped for a quick lunch in a Chinese restaurant on

44

Cowper Street and then drove over to the Criminal Courts Building on High Street. The Supreme Court judge to whom they presented their written request sounded dubious about granting them the order solely on the basis of a telephone conversation with a security guard, but Carella pointed out that there was reasonable cause to believe that *someone* who'd announced himself as Daniel Corbett had been at the scene during the hours the crime was committed and that time was of the essence in locating the stolen jewelry before it was disposed of. They argued it back and forth for perhaps fifteen minutes. At the end of that time the judge said, "Officer, I simply cannot agree that you have reasonable cause to conduct a search. Were I to grant this order, it would only be disputed later, when your case comes to trial. Application denied." Carella mumbled to himself all the way out to the elevators and all the way down to the street. Hawes commented that one of the nice things about living in a democracy was that a citizen's rights were so carefully protected, and Carella said, "A *criminal's* rights, too," and that was that.

They struck out with Jerry Mandel as well. A call to the Three Oaks Lodge in Mount Semanee informed them that he had checked out that morning, looking for better skiing conditions elsewhere. Carella told the desk clerk that if Mandel wanted snow, they were up to their eyeballs in it right here in the city. By then six inches had fallen, and it was still coming down. The clerk said, "Ship some of it up here; we can use it."

Carella hung up.

4

The first of the crank calls came at two-thirty that afternoon, proving to Carella's satisfaction that not only every *author* on the face of the earth received them, but perhaps every *cop* as well. The caller was a woman who said her name was Miss Betty Aldershot, and she said she lived at 782 Jackson, just across the street from the Harborview complex. She said that at exactly twenty-five minutes to seven on Thursday night, she'd been looking through her window at the street below when she saw a man and a woman struggling in the snow. Carella did not know this was a crank call; not just *yet* he didn't. He shoved a pad into place on his desk and picked up a pencil.

"Yes, Miss Aldershot, I'm listening," he said. "Can you describe the man to me?"

"He was Superman," she said.

"Superman?"

"Yes. He was wearing blue underwear and a red cape."

"I see," Carella said.

"He took out a big red penis and stuck it in her."

"I see."

"A *superman* penis," she said.

"Uh-huh. Well, Mrs. Aldershot, thank you for . . ."

"Then he flew away."

"Uh-huh."

"Up over the buildings. It was still hanging out."

"Uh-huh. Well, fine, thanks a lot."

"You'll never get him," she said, and began cackling. "He can go faster than a speeding bullet," and she hung up.

"Who was that?" Meyer Meyer said from his desk. He was wearing the hat he had taken to wearing indoors and out, a checked deerstalker that hid his bald head and made him feel like Sherlock Holmes. The men in the squadroom had been speculating only a week ago about whether or not he wore it to bed. Hal Willis suggested that Meyer's wife, Sarah, liked to get shtupped by baldheaded men wearing deerstalker hats. Deerstalker hats and black garters, Bert Kling said. Nothing else. Just the deerstalker hat and the black garters. And a big hard-on, Hawes said. Very funny, Meyer said.

"That was Superman's mother," Carella said.

"Yeah? How's she doing?"

"Terrific. I've been trying to reach Danny Gimp. Has he changed his number or something?"

"Not that I know of," Meyer said. "Listen, what are we going to do about Monday?"

"I expect to crack this case by midnight tonight," Carella said.

"Sure, you and Superman. Seriously. If you plan to be shlepping all over the city, then let me have Chanukah."

"Give me till midnight," Carella said, and tried Danny Gimp's number again. Still no answer. He disliked doing business with Fats Donner, but there was more than eighty-three thousand dollars' worth of hot jewels floating around out there in the city, and such a haul might not have gone unnoticed in the underworld. He dialed Donner's home number and listened to it ringing on the other end.

"Donner," a voice said.

"Fats, this is Detective Carella."

"Hey, how are you?" Donner said. "What's up?" His voice was unctuous and oily; it conjured for Carella the mountainous, blubbery man who was Hal Willis's favorite informer— but that was only because Willis had enough on him to send him away for the next twenty years. Fats Donner had a penchant for young girls, a charming obsession that caused him constantly to skirt the thin ice outside the law. Carella visualized his thick fingers holding the telephone receiver; he imagined those same fingers on the budding breasts of a thirteen-year-old. The man revolted him, but murder revolted him more.

"Something like eighty-three thousand dollars in jewelry was stolen Thursday night during the commission of a homicide," Carella said. "Hear anything about it?"

Donner whistled softly. Or perhaps it was only a wheeze. "What kind of stuff?" he asked.

"A mixed bag, I'll read you the list in a minute. In the meantime, has there been any rumble on it?"

"Nothing I heard," Donner said. "Thursday night, you say?"

"The twenty-first."

"This is Saturday. Could be it's already been fenced."

"Could be."

47

"Let me go on the earie," Donner said. "This'll cost you, though."

"You can discuss price with Willis," Carella said.

"Willis is a tightwad. This is Christmastime; I got presents to buy. *I'm* human, too, you know. You're asking me to go out in the snow and listen around when I should be home instead, putting up my tree."

"For all your little kiddies?" Carella asked, and the line went silent.

"Well, okay, I'll discuss price with Willis. But I want something even if I don't score. This is Christmastime."

"Discuss it with Willis," Carella said, and read off the list of stolen items.

"That's a whole lot of shit there," Donner said. "I'll see what I can do," and hung up.

Carella tried Danny Gimp again. Still no answer. He debated calling Gaucho Palacios, but he didn't think something as big as this would reach the Cowboy's ears. The clock on the squadroom wall read ten minutes to three. He didn't know what the hell to do next. He couldn't run a lineup on Corbett until Mandel got back to the city on the day after Christmas. He couldn't get a court order to search Corbett's apartment for the stolen jewelry, and he couldn't get a line on the jewelry until Donner got back to him—*if* he got back to him. He went down the hall to Clerical and asked Miscolo to mimeograph copies of the jewelry list for distribution to the city's pawnshops, but he knew damn well they'd all be closed tomorrow and Monday, which put him almost into Tuesday, when Mandel would be back. At his own desk again, he dialed the Three Oaks Lodge in Mount Semanee and asked to talk to the manager. It was still snowing. Across the room, Cotton Hawes was working up a timetable for the Thursday night murders. Carella waited.

"Hello?" a woman's voice said.

"Hello, this is Detective Carella of the Eighty-seventh Squad in Isola," Carella said. "I spoke to someone there a little while ago, and he told me that Jerry Mandel had checked out early this morning . . ."

"Yes?"

"The person I spoke to said he had no idea where Mr. Mandel was heading. I was wondering . . ."

"I have no idea either," the woman said.

"Who is this, please?"

"Mrs. Carmody, the manager."

"Mrs. Carmody, has there been any substantial snowfall in the state over the past several days?"

"Not in the state, no. I understand it's snowing there in the city . . ."

"Yes, right now, in fact."

"Well, maybe we'll get some of it later today. I *hope*," she said.

"Where would the nearest area with snow be?"

"From Semanee, do you mean?"

"Yes. If Mr. Mandel was looking for snow, where would he have found it?"

"Not before Vermont," Mrs. Carmody said.

"Vermont."

"Yes. Mount Snow was reporting excellent conditions, as were Bromely, Stratton, Sugarbush, and Stowe. We've been desperate for snow here, and so has Massachusetts. My guess is he'd have headed for Vermont."

"Where in Vermont? Which area would be the closest to Semanee?"

"Mount Snow."

"Is that a very busy area? Are there many motels there?"

"You've got to be joking," Mrs. Carmody said. "Were you thinking of trying to track him down?"

"It crossed my mind," Carella said.

"If you started calling all the hotels at Mount Snow right this minute, you'd miss Santa coming down the chimney," she said, and he was sure she was smiling at her own witticism.

"How do I get a complete listing of all the available lodging there?" Carella asked.

"Are you serious?"

"Yes, ma'am, we're investigating a murder here."

"Well . . . I guess you can call the Mount Snow Lodging Bureau. Maybe they can help you."

"Thank you," Carella said, and hung up.

Hawes came over to the desk with the timetable he'd been typing.

"This is the way it looks to me," he said, and handed the sheet to Carella:

```
    TIMETABLE—CRAIG AND ESPOSITO MURDERS
            THURSDAY, DECEMBER 21

5:00 P.M.    Man claiming to be Daniel Cor-
             bett  arrives  at  Harborview,
```

	goes up in elevator after being announced by security guard Mandel.
6:15 P.M.	Man has still not left building when Karlson relieves Mandel at the door.
6:40 P.M.	Call to Emergency 911 from unidentified male reporting cutting victim on sidewalk outside 781 Jackson Street.
6:43 P.M.	Car Adam Eleven responds, woman later identified as Marian Esposito, white female, thirty-two years old, DOA.
7:10 P.M.	Call to Emergency 911 from Hillary Scott reporting stabbing in Apartment 304 at 781 Jackson.
7:14 P.M.	Detectives already on scene of Esposito murder respond. Victim Gregory Craig, white male, fifty-four years old, DOA.

"That's about it, all right," Carella said.

"Doesn't tell us a damn thing, does it?" Hawes said.

"Not much," Carella said, "but it's nice to have it all spelled out every now and then." He picked up the phone, dialed the operator, and asked for Vermont Information. She told him he could dial that direct, and he testily informed her he was a detective investigating a homicide, and he'd appreciate it if she could get it for him. She said, sarcastically, "Oh, I *beg* your pardon," but she connected him nonetheless. Vermont Information gave him the listing for the Mount Snow Lodging Bureau, and he dialed that number direct and spoke to a nice young woman, who informed him that there were fifty-six hotels, motels, inns, and lodges listed with the Bureau, all within a twenty-mile radius of Mount Snow. She mentioned in passing that the Bureau did not list any hostelry with fewer than four rooms, of which there were a great many. She asked if he wanted her to read off the entire list, together wth the capacity for each place.

Carella debated this for a moment.

Then he said, "No, never mind, thanks," and hung up.

The second crank call—or so it seemed at first—came twenty minutes after the first one. He lifted the receiver from its cradle and said, "Eighty-seventh Squad, Carella."

"It has something to do with water," a woman's voice said.

"What?"

"Water," the voice repeated, and suddenly he recognized her.

"Miss Scott?" he said.

"Yes. The murder has to do with water. Can I see you this afternoon? You're the source."

"What do you mean?"

"I'm not sure yet. But you're the source. I have to talk to you."

He remembered what Gregory Craig's daughter had told them yesterday: *She drowned. They said it was an accident.* Water, he thought, and said at once, "Where will you be?"

"At my sister's," she said.

"Give me half an hour," he said.

"I'll see you there," she said, and hung up.

When she opened the door for him, she was wearing a short robe belted over either pantyhose or nylons. She wore no makeup; without lipstick, rouge, or liner, she resembled Teddy even more than she had before.

"I'm sorry," she said at once. "I was dressing when my sister called. Come in."

The apartment was in the Stewart City section of Isola. Stewart City was not really a city, or even a town, but merely a collection of swank apartment buildings overlooking the River Dix on the true city's south side. If you could boast of a Stewart City address, you could also boast of a high income, a country place on Sands Spit, and a Mercedes-Benz in the garage under your building. You could give your address with a measure of snobbery and pride. There were few places left in the city—or perhaps the world—where you could do the same. Denise Scott's apartment, as befitted its location, was decorated expensively but not ostentatiously; it had the effect on Carella of making him feel immediately uncomfortable. The cool white artificial Christmas tree in one corner of the room compounded his sense of ill ease. He was accustomed to the scuzziness of the Eight-Seven, where the Christmas trees were real and the carpeting underfoot—unlike the *lawn* growing in this place—was more often than not tattered and frayed.

51

"Miss Scott," he said, "on the phone, you . . ."

"Is it still snowing out there?" she asked.

"Yes."

"I'm supposed to be downtown at five for a cocktail party. Are there any cabs on the street?"

"A few."

"Can I get you a drink?" she asked. "What time is it anyway?"

"Four o'clock," he said.

"That's not too early for a drink, is it?"

"I can't," he said.

"Right, you're on duty," she said. "Mind if I have one?"

"Go right ahead."

She went to a tall cabinet on the wall opposite the tree and opened both doors of it to reveal an array of bottles within. She poured generously from one of the bottles, took two ice cubes from a bucket, and dropped them into the glass. Turning to him, she said, "Cheers, happy holidays."

"Cheers," he said.

"Sit down," she said. "Please." Her smile was so similar to Teddy's that he found himself experiencing an odd sense of disorientation. The woman in this apartment should have been in his Riverhead house instead. He should have been telling her about the hard day's work he'd put in, soliciting sympathy for the policeman's lot; he should have been mixing her a scotch and soda and laying a fire for her on the hearth. Instead, he was here to talk about water.

"So," he said, "what about water?"

She looked at him, puzzled, and then said, "Thanks, I prefer it on the rocks."

He looked back at her, equally puzzled. She sat in the chair opposite him, the robe falling away as she crossed her legs. She rearranged the wayward flap at once.

"Are you sure you won't have one?" she asked.

"Positive."

"She may be awhile, you know."

"I'm sorry, what . . . ?"

"My sister. I spoke to her half an hour ago."

"Your sister?"

"Yes."

"What's *she* got to do . . . ?"

"Hillary," she said.

"Hillary?" he said, and blinked. The lady, as he'd surmised from the very beginning, was a prime candidate for the loony bin. "Miss Scott," he said, "I'm sorry, but I don't understand what . . ."

"My twin sister," she said.

He looked at her. She was smiling over the rim of her glass. He had the feeling she had done this many times before and enjoyed doing it each and every time.

"I see," he said.

"I'm Denise," she said. "We look a lot alike, don't you think?"

"Yes, you do," he said cautiously, wondering whether there really *was* a twin sister or whether Hillary was just having a little sport with him at the city's expense. "You say you spoke to her . . ."

"Yes, half an hour ago."

"Where was she?"

"At the office. She was just leaving. But with this snow . . ."

"Listen," he said, "are you *really* . . . ?"

"Denise Scott," she said, "yes," and nodded. "Which of us do you think is prettiest?"

"I couldn't say, Miss Scott."

"*I* am," she said, and giggled, and rose suddenly, and went to the liquor cabinet. He watched as she poured herself another drink. "Are you sure?" she asked, and lifted the glass to him.

"I'm sorry, I can't."

"Pity," she said, and went back to her chair and sat again. She crossed her legs more recklessly this time. The flap of the robe fell open again, and he saw the gartered tops of nylon stockings. He glanced away.

"I have twins myself," he said.

"Yes, Hillary told me."

"I never mentioned to her . . ."

"Psychic, you know," Denise said, and tapped her temple with her forefinger.

"How about you?" he said.

"No, no, my talents run in other directions," she said, and smiled at him. "Aren't you glad garter belts are coming back?" she said.

"I've . . . never much thought about it," he said.

"Think about it," she said.

"Miss Scott," he said, "I know you have an appointment, so if you want to get dressed, I'll be perfectly all right here."

"Wouldn't *dream* of leaving you alone," she said, and

suddenly bent over the coffee table to spear a cigarette from the container there. The upper half of the robe gapped open over her breasts. She was wearing no bra. She held the pose an instant longer than she needed to, reaching for the cigarette, looking up at him and suddenly smiling.

"Miss Scott," he said, rising. "I'll be back in a little while. When your sister gets here, tell her . . ."

He heard a key turning in the door behind him. The door swung wide, and Hillary Scott came into the room. She was wearing a raccoon coat open over a white blouse and a red skirt. Her dark brown boots were wet. She looked across the room to where Denise was still bent over the coffee table. "Go put on some clothes," she said. "You'll catch cold." To Carella, she said, "I'm sorry I'm late. I had a hell of a time getting a cab." She looked at her sister again. "Denise?"

"Nice meeting you," Denise said, and rose, and tucked one flap of the robe over the other, and tightened the belt. He watched her as she left the room. The door to what he assumed was the bedroom whispered shut behind her.

"Didn't know there were *three* of us, did you?" Hillary said.

"Three of you?"

"Including your wife."

"You've never met my wife," Carella said.

"But we resemble each other."

"Yes."

"You have twins."

"Yes."

"The little girl looks like your wife. She was born in April."

"No, but that's her name."

"Terry. Is it Terry?"

"Teddy."

"Yes, Teddy. Franklin? Was her maiden name Franklin?"

"Yes," he said. He was staring at her unbelievingly. "Miss Scott," he said, "on the phone you told me . . ."

"Yes, water."

"What *about* water?"

"Something to do with water. Did someone mention water to you recently?"

Beyond the bedroom door he heard either a radio or a record player erupting with a rock tune. Hillary turned impatiently toward the door and shouted, "Denise, turn that down!" She waited a moment, the music blaring, and then

54

shouted, *"Denise!"* just as the music dropped six decibels. Angrily she took a cigarette from the container on the table, put a match to it, and let out a stream of smoke. "We'll wait till she's gone," she said. "It's impossible to achieve any level of concentration with her here. Would you like a drink?"

"No, thank you."

"I think *I'll* have one," she said, and went to the cabinet, and poured a hefty shot of whiskey into a tumbler, and drank it almost in one gulp. Carella suddenly remembered the Craig autopsy report.

"Was Craig a heavy drinker?" he asked.

"Why do you want to know?"

"The autopsy report indicated he'd been drinking before his death."

"I wouldn't say he was a heavy drinker, no."

"Social drinker?"

"Two or three before dinner."

"Did he drink while he was working?"

"Never."

In the next ten minutes, while her sister dressed in the other room, Hillary consumed two more healthy glasses of whiskey, presumably the better to heighten her psychic awareness. Carella wondered what the hell he was doing here. Take a phone call from a crazy lady who claimed to be psychic, link it foolishly to a drowning in Massachusetts that happened three years ago, and then wait around while the clock ticked steadily and the snow kept falling and the whiskey content in the bottle got lower and lower. But she had known his wife's name without being told it, knew they had twins, almost zeroed in on April. He did not for a moment believe she could actually read minds, but he knew that people with extrasensory perception did possibly exist, and he was not about to dismiss her earlier reference to water. Gregory Craig's wife had drowned three years ago— and his daughter could not believe it was an accident.

The bedroom door opened.

Denise Scott was wearing a clinging green jersey dress slit outrageously wide over her breasts and held precariously together at the midriff with a diamond clasp the size of Taiwan. The dress was somewhat shorter than was fashionable these days, giving her legs an extraordinarily long and supple look. She was wearing green high-heeled satin pumps; Carella gave them a life expectancy of thirty seconds in the snow outside. She walked to the hall closet without saying a word, took off the pumps, zipped on a pair of black leather

55

boots, took a long black coat from the closet, picked up a black velvet bag from the hall table, tucked the pumps under her arm, opened the door, grinned at Carella, said, "Another time, *amigo*," and walked out without saying good-bye to Hillary.

"Bitch," Hillary said, and poured herself another drink.

"Go easy on that, okay?" Carella said.

"Tried to take Greg away from me," she said. "Went to the apartment one afternoon while he was working, pulled the twin-sister routine on him. I found her naked in bed with him." She shook her head and took a swift swallow of whiskey.

"When was this?" he asked at once. She had just presented him with the best possible motive for murder. In this city, the homicide statistics changed as often as the police changed their underwear, but the swing was back to "personal" murders as opposed to the "impersonal" ones that had screamed across the headlines just several years back. The good old-fashioned slayings were now in vogue again: husbands shooting wives and vice versa, lovers taking axes to rivals, sons stabbing mothers and sisters; your average garden-variety homespun killings. Hillary Scott had found Gregory Craig in bed with her own sister.

"When?" he asked again.

"When what?"

"When did you discover them together?"

"Last month sometime."

"November?"

"November."

"What happened?"

"Little nympho bitch," Hillary said.

"What happened? What did you do?"

"Told her if she ever came near that apartment again . . ." She shook her head. "My own sister. Said it was a joke, said she wanted to see if Greg could tell us apart."

"Could he?"

"He said he thought she was me. He said she fooled him completely."

"What did *you* think?"

"I think he knew."

"But you're here with her now."

"What?"

"You're staying with her. Even after what happened."

"I didn't talk to her for weeks. Then she called one day in tears and . . . she's my sister. We're closer than any two

56

people in the world. We're *twins*. What could I do?"

He understood this completely. Despite their constant bickering, his own twins were inseparable. Listening to their running dialogues was like listening to one person talking out loud to himself. When both of them were engaged in make-believe together, it was sometimes impossible to break in on what amounted to a tandem stream of consciousness. He had read someplace that twins were a gang in miniature; he had understood the writer's allusion at once. He had once scolded Mark for carelessly breaking an expensive vase and had punished him by sending him to his room. Ten minutes later he had found April in her room. When he'd mentioned to her that *she* wasn't the one being punished, April had said, "Well, I just thought I'd help him out." If there was any truth to the adage that blood ran thicker than water, it ran doubly thick between twins. Hillary had found her sister in bed with Gregory Craig, but Craig was the stranger, and Denise was her twin. And now Craig was dead.

"How'd that affect your relationship with him?" Carella asked.

"I trusted him less. But I still loved him. If you love somebody, you're willing to forgive a lapse or two."

Carella nodded. He supposed she was telling the truth, but he wondered at the same time how *he'd* have felt if he'd found Teddy in bed with his twin brother, if he *had* a twin brother or any brother at all, which he didn't have.

"What's this about water?" he said. "You told me on the phone . . ."

"Someone mentioned water to you, am I right?"

"Yes, someone did."

"Something about water. And biting."

She drowned in the Bight, Abigail Craig had told him, *two miles from where my father was renting his famous haunted house.*

"What else?" Carella asked.

"Bite," she said.

"Yes, what about it?"

"Give me your hands."

He held out his hands to her. They stood a foot apart from each other, facing each other, their hands clasped. She closed her eyes.

"Someone swimming," she said. "A woman. Tape. So strong. I feel it pulsing in your hands. Tape. No, I'm *losing* it," she said abruptly, and opened her eyes wide. "Concentrate! You're the source!" She squeezed his hands tightly and closed her eyes again. "Yes," she said, the word coming out like a hiss. She was breathing harshly now; her hands in his own were trembling. "Drowning. Tape. Drowning, drowning," she said, and suddenly released his hands and threw her arms around him, her eyes still closed, her own hands clasping him behind the neck. He tried to back away from her, but her lips found his, and her mouth drew at him as though trying to suck the breath from his body. Hissing, she clamped her teeth onto his lower lip, and he pushed her away at once. She stood there with her eyes closed, her entire body shaking. She seemed unaware of him now. She began to sway, and then suddenly she began talking in a voice quite unlike her own, a hollow sepulchral voice that seemed to rumble up from the depths of some forgotten bog, trailing tatters of mist and a wind as cold as the grave.

"You stole," she said. "I know, I heard, you stole, I know, I'll tell," she said, "you stole, you stole . . ."

Her voice trailed. The room was silent except for the ticking of the clock. She stood there swaying, her eyes still closed, but the trembling was gone now, and at last the swaying stopped, too, and she was utterly motionless for several moments. She opened her eyes then and seemed surprised to find him there.

"I . . . have to rest," she said. "Please go."

She left him alone in the room. The door to the bedroom eased shut behind him. He stood there watching the closed door for a moment, and then he put on his coat and left the apartment.

The Carella house in Riverhead was a huge white elephant they'd picked up for a song—well, more accurately a five-act opera—shortly after the twins were born. Teddy's father had presented them with a registered nurse as a month-long gift while Teddy was recuperating after the birth, and Fanny Knowles had elected to stay on with them later at a salary they could afford, telling them she was tired of taking care of sick old men all the time. Without her, they'd never have been able to manage the big old house—or the twins either, for that matter. Fanny was "fiftyish," as she put it, and she had blue hair, and she wore pince-nez, and she weighed 150 pounds, and she ran the Carella household with the same sort of Irish bullheadedness the gang foremen must have displayed when immigrants were digging the city's subway system at the turn of the century. It was Fanny who absolutely refused to take into the house a stray Labrador retriever Carella had adopted while investigating the murders of a blind man and his wife. She told him simply and flatly that there was enough to do around here without having to clean up after a big old hound. She was fond of saying, prophetically in this case, "I take no shit from man nor beast," an expression the ten-year-old twins had picked up when they were still learning to talk and which Mark now used with more frequency than April. The twins' speech patterns, in fact—much to Carella's consternation—were more closely modeled after Fanny's than anyone else's; it was *her* voice they heard around the house whenever Carella wasn't home.

There seemed to be no one at *all* home when he unlocked the front door. It had taken him an hour and a half to make the trip from Stewart City to Riverhead in blinding snow over treacherous roads; it normally would have taken him forty minutes. He had struggled to get the car up his driveway, had given up after six runs at it, and had finally parked it at the curb, behind Mr. Henderson's car next door, already partially covered with drifts. He stood outside the front door now and stamped the snow from his shoes before entering. The house was silent. He turned on the entrance-hall lights, hung his coat on the pearwood coatrack just inside the door, and shouted, "Hi, anybody home?" There was no answer.

The grandfather clock that had also been a gift from Teddy's father chimed the half hour. It was six-thirty. He knew Teddy and Fanny had taken the twins to see Santa—as *he* was supposed to have done today—but they should have been home by now, even with the storm. He switched on the floor lamp near the piano and the Tiffany-style lamp on the end table near the sofa and then walked through the living room into the kitchen. He took a tray of ice cubes from the freezer compartment, went back into the living room, and was mixing himself a drink at the bar unit when the telephone rang. He snatched the receiver from the cradle at once.

"Hello?" he said.

"Steve, it's Fanny."

"Yes, Fanny, where are you?"

"We're stuck downtown here outside Coopersmith's. It's the devil getting a cab; there just aren't any to be found. We're thinking of taking a train to the Gladiola Station—if we can get crosstown from here."

"How about the subway?"

"The T. R. and L. is closer, if we can get to it. It may be awhile, though. I'll call you as soon as I know what we'll be doing."

"How was Santa Claus?"

"A dirty old man with a fake beard. Go fix yourself a drink," Fanny said, and hung up.

He put down the receiver and went back to the bar unit, wondering when Fanny had developed psychic powers of her own. His lip felt bruised from Hillary's trance-induced mouth-to-mouth resuscitation in reverse. He had not kissed another woman since the day he married Teddy, nor did he feel he'd kissed one now. Whatever had transpired in the living room of Denise Scott's apartment had been robbed of all sexuality by the fierceness of Hillary's quest. She might just as well have been pressing a necromancer's stone to her mouth, and he'd been frightened, rather than aroused, fearful that she truly did possess a power that would drain his soul from the shell of his body and leave it a quivering gray mass on the carpet at his feet. He had every intention of telling Teddy what had happened the moment she got home. He wondered when the hell that would be, stirred himself a martini, very dry, and then plopped two olives into the glass. He was turning on the Christmas tree lights when the phone rang.

"Steve, it's me again," Fanny said. "This is hopeless. We're going to have to look for a hotel someplace."

"Where are you now?"

"On Waverly and Dome. We walked here from Coopersmith's. The twins are freezing; they were both wearing only ski parkas when we left the house this morning."

"Waverly and Dome," he said. "Try the Waverly Plaza; it should be right around the corner from you. And call me back when you're settled, will you?"

"Yes, fine."

"I'll be here by the phone."

"Have you had a drink yet?"

"Yes, Fanny."

"Good. That's the first thing *I'm* going to do when we find a bloody place to stay."

"Call me back."

"I will," she said, and hung up.

He went to the fireplace, tore yesterday's newspaper—the one with Gregory Craig's obit in it—into strips, and tossed them under the grate. He piled his kindling carefully on top of the shredded newspaper, stacked three logs on top of that, and struck a match. He was on his second martini when the phone rang again. It was Fanny reporting that they had managed to get two rooms at the Waverly, which they wouldn't have got if she hadn't pulled rank and told them that the poor shivering darlings over there were the wife and children of Detective Stephen Louis Carella of the Eighty-seventh Precinct. He had never considered himself a man with any clout, but apparently his being a city detective had got Fanny and his family a pair of rooms for the night.

"Do you want to say hello to the kids?" she asked.

"Yes, put them on, please."

"They're next door, watching television. Just a second."

He heard her calling to the twins through what was obviously the door to connecting rooms. April came on the line first.

"Daddy," she said, "Mark won't let me watch my show."

"Tell him I said you can watch your show for an hour, and then he can watch his."

"I never saw so much snow in my *life*," April said. "We're not going to have to spend *Christmas* here, are we?"

"No, darling. Put Mark on, will you?"

"Just a second. I love you, Daddy."

"Love you, too," he said, and waited.

"Hi," Mark said.

"Let her watch for an hour, and then you can put on whatever you want, okay?" Carella said.

"Yeah, okay. I guess."

"Everything all right now?"

"Fanny ordered a double Manhattan from room service."

"Good. How about Mom?"

"She's drinking scotch. We almost froze to death, Dad."

"Tell her I love her. I'll call in the morning, okay? What are your room numbers?"

"Six-oh-three and six-oh-four."

"Okay, son, sleep tight."

"We're not going to bed *yet*," Mark said.

"When you do."

"Okay, Dad."

Carella put the receiver back on the cradle. He finished his drink, and then cooked himself some hot dogs and baked beans, and warmed a jar of sauerkraut, and ate off a paper plate before the fire, sipping at a bottle of beer. He cleaned up the kitchen afterward and went to bed at nine-thirty. It was the first time he'd ever slept alone in this house. He kept thinking of what had happened with Hillary earlier today. *Someone swimming. A woman. Tape. Drowning. Tape. Drowning. You stole. I heard. I know. I'll tell.*

His lip still ached.

61

5

He didn't know quite what to do about switching back with Meyer. He had no desire to deprive him of his holiday, but at the same time he knew a door-to-door canvass of the Harborview building might prove an empty exercise tomorrow, when many of the tenants might be off sharing Christmas/ Chanukah with people elsewhere in the city. He decided to hit the building today, and the first call he made—from home—was to Meyer.

Sarah answered the telephone. She told him her husband was in the shower and asked if he could return the call when he got out. Carella said he'd be there for another hour at least. He was already wondering how he'd get to work this morning; his car was still at the curb under what looked like seven tons of snow. He hung up and called Hawes at home.

"Cotton," he said, "I want to hit that building today."

"Okay," Hawes said.

"There are twelve floors, five apartments on each floor. If we split them between us, that gives each of us thirty apartments. Figure an average of fifteen minutes for each stop, we'll be putting in an eight-hour day, more or less."

Hawes, who was not too good at arithmetic, said, "Yeah, more or less."

"You can go over there whenever you like," Carella said. "I'll be leaving here in an hour or so."

"Okay," Hawes said.

"You want to start at the bottom or the top?"

"My father told me to always start at the top."

"Okay, fine, I'll work my way up. Let's plan on a lunch break at about one. I'll meet you in the lobby."

"Right," Hawes said, and hung up.

Carella was himself in the shower when he heard the phone ringing. He turned off the water, grabbed a towel, ran out into the bedroom, and caught the phone on the sixth ring. Meyer was on the other end.

"I was in the shower," Carella told him.

"We have to stop meeting in the shower," Meyer said. "The fellas are beginning to talk."

"I was calling about tomorrow."

"Yeah, what do you think?"

"I'll have to hit that building today."

"Okay."

"I'm sorry, Meyer."

"Listen, *you* didn't kill those people," Meyer said. "How do you like the snow? Is it a white enough Christmas for you? How are you getting downtown?"

"By subway, I guess."

"Like the poor people," Meyer said. "Listen, don't worry about tomorrow, okay? That was our original deal anyway."

The floor-by-floor, door-to-door canvass of 781 Jackson took Carella and Hawes a bit less time than they'd expected. Carella reached the building at a little after ten, a half hour after Hawes had already started on the top floor. They broke for lunch at one, as they'd arranged, and were through for the day at four-thirty. They stopped for coffee and crullers at a greasy spoon near the building and went over their notes together. It would later take each of them several hours to type up a collaborative report in quintuplicate from the notes they'd individually made. One copy of the report would go to Lieutenant Byrnes. Another copy would go to Captain Frick, who was in command of the entire precinct. The third copy would go to Homicide, and the remaining two copies would be filed respectively in the Craig and Esposito case folders. Normally, there would have been only four copies, but this was a case with a companion case, and vice versa.

They had, until now, thought of the Esposito murder as the *true* companion case, despite the cross-indexing that labeled the Craig murder a companion case as well. Now they began to look at things in a somewhat different light. They were both experienced cops, and they knew all about smoke-screen murders. One of Carella's earliest cases—this was before Hawes had joined the squad, even before Carella and Teddy were married, in fact—had seemed to focus on a cop hater who was running around shooting policemen. But that had been only the smoke-screen; the killer had really been after a *specific* cop and was spreading vapor to mist over the true purpose. Before Hawes's transfer to the Eight-Seven, he'd investigated a case in which the killer had chopped off the hands of his victim and then killed two other people elsewhere in the city and chopped off *their* hands as well. He was after insurance money, and he'd chopped off his true quarry's

63

hands because he didn't want a fingerprint identification that would have disqualified the claim. The second and third murders were smoke-screen murders, designed to lead the cops into believing they were looking for some kind of freak who went around dismembering his victims.

They would not have thought, until now, that the murder of Gregory Craig was a smoke screen for the murder of Marian Esposito. Everything seemed to indicate that the second murder was a murder of expedience—the killer fleeing from the building with a bloody knife in his hands perhaps, and being seen, and panicking at the possibility of later identification. Zzzzaaaahhhh went the knife, and zing went the strings of my heart. But now they wondered. They wondered because three separate tenants of 781 Jackson told them that Marian and Warren Esposito shared a marriage that could at best be termed rocky.

The couple who lived next door to the Espositos—in Apartment 702, one of the apartments Hawes hit—told him that on two separate occasions Marian had called the police because her husband was beating her up. On each of those occasions the responding patrolmen had settled, on the scene, what is euphemistically known to the police as "a family dispute." But Marian walked around with a pair of black eyes for weeks after the first beating, and her nose was broken during the second beating.

The tenant in Apartment 508—who recognized Marian from the somewhat unflattering picture the Photo Unit had taken at the scene—told Carella that he'd been riding up in the elevator one time with the Espositos, and they'd started arguing about something, and Warren Esposito had grabbed his wife's arm and twisted it violently behind her back. "Thought sure he'd break it," the man said, and then offered Carella a glass of wine, which Carella refused. The man was waiting for his son and daughter-in-law to come visit him for the holiday. His wife had died six months ago; this was to be his first Christmas without her. He again offered Carella a glass of wine. Carella had to refuse; he was a cop on duty. But he lingered longer than the fifteen minutes he'd allotted for each apartment, sensing the old man's loneliness and hoping to hell his son and daughter-in-law would not disappoint him.

In Apartment 601, just below the Esposito apartment, the woman tenant there told Carella that there was always a lot of yelling and thumping going on upstairs, sometimes at two, three in the morning. She was wrapping Christmas gifts at her kitchen table as she disclosed the information. "Sometimes," she said, and carefully tied a bow, "if there are children living above you, there'll be a lot of running around and noise. But the Espositos have no children. And of course, everybody in the building knows he beats her." She picked up the scissors and gingerly snipped off the end of the ribbon.

"So it looks like we've got a wife beater," Hawes said.

"Looks that way."

"Came in yesterday wanting to know what we were doing to find his wife's murderer," Hawes said, and shook his head. "Had his lawyer call the lieutenant to turn on the screws. He must miss having her to bat around."

"I want to check this with Records, see if she really *did* call us twice," Carella said. "Have you got some change?"

Hawes dug in his pocket and came up with a handful of coins. Carella plucked two dimes from his palm and then went to the phone booth near the cigarette machine. At one of the other tables a blonde in her forties, wearing a sprig of holly on the collar of her coat, turned to Hawes and smiled at him. He smiled back. Carella was on the phone only long enough to get the information he needed. When he got back to the table, he said, "It checks out. First call was on August eighteenth; second one was November twelfth. I'd like to talk to Esposito right now, what do you say?"

"I'm bushed," Hawes said. "But if he's our man, I don't want him spending Christmas in South America."

They knocked on the door to the Esposito apartment at ten minutes to five. Warren Esposito opened the door for them when he recognized Hawes through the peephole. He was wearing only trousers and a tank-top undershirt. He told them he was dressing to go back to the funeral parlor. He said he'd been there all afternoon and had come home to shower and change his clothes. His eyes were puffy and red; it was evident he'd been crying. Carella remembered Hillary Scott's description of the "ghost" who'd slain Gregory Craig. Warren Esposito was perhaps thirty-four years old, with curly black hair and dark brown eyes. But how many *other* people were there in this city with that same combination of hair and eyes, including someone who'd announced himself as Daniel Corbett to the security guard on the day of the murders—and besides, who the hell believed in either mediums *or* ghosts?

Warren Esposito was no poltergeist. He was perhaps six feet two inches tall, slightly taller than Carella and just as tall as Hawes, with muscles bulging all over his chest, his biceps, and his forearms. The woman Carella had seen lying dead on the sidewalk was perhaps five feet six inches tall, and he guessed she must have weighed about 115 pounds. *Nice man, Mr. Muscles Esposito,* Carella thought, and asked his first question.

"Mr. Esposito," he said, "is it true that on two separate occasions your wife phoned the police for assistance in a family dispute?"

"Where'd you hear that?" Esposito said. "The people in this building ought to mind their own business. Who was it? Kruger next door?"

"The patrolmen responding to both calls made full reports," Carella said.

"Well . . . there may have been one or two arguments," Esposito said.

"And your wife called the police, right?"

"Yes, I suppose she did."

"During one of those arguments did you blacken both her eyes?"

"Who told you that?"

"It's in the report," Carella said.

"We were arguing, that's all."

"Did you blacken her eyes?"

"I may have."

"And on the second occasion did you break her nose?"

"Maybe."

"Did you once twist her arm so violently that a witness thought you'd surely broken it?"

"I know who *that* is," Esposito said. "That's Di Luca down on the fifth floor, isn't it? Boy, I wish these goddamn people would mind their own business."

"Did you, or didn't you?"

"I suppose so. What difference does it make? What is it you're trying to say, Mr. Carella? Are you trying to say I *killed* her? Just because we *argued* every now and then? Don't you argue with *your* wife? Are you married?"

"I'm married," Carella said.

"So don't you and your wife . . . ?"

"Let's talk about you and *your* wife, okay?" Carella said.

"Where were you between six and seven P.M. on Thursday night?" Hawes asked.

"Listen," Esposito said, "if this is going to turn into a third degree here, I want to call my lawyer."

"You don't need a lawyer to answer a few questions," Hawes said.

"Not unless the questions make it sound like I killed my wife."

"Only the answers can do that."

"I want to call my lawyer."

"Okay, call your lawyer," Carella said. "Tell him we're asking you some simple questions you refuse to answer, and tell him we may have to get those answers before a grand jury. Go ahead, call him."

"A grand jury? What the hell . . . ?"

"A grand jury, yes. Call your lawyer."

"I will."

"I wish you would. We're wasting time here."

Esposito went to the phone and dialed a number. He listened as the phone rang and then said, "Joyce, this is Warren Esposito. Is Jerry there? Thank you." He waited again, and then said into the phone, "Jerry, I've got two detectives here, and they're asking questions about where I *was* Thursday, and threatening me with a grand jury . . . sure, just a second." He held out the phone to Carella. "He wants to talk to one of you."

Carella took the phone. "Hello?" he said.

"Who's this?" the voice on the other end said.

"Detective Carella, Eighty-seventh Squad. Who's this?"

"Jerome Lieberman, Mr. Esposito's attorney. I understand you've been threatening my client with a grand jury if he . . ."

"No one's been threatening anybody, Mr. Lieberman. We wanted to ask some questions, and he wanted to call his lawyer. So he called you, and here you are."

"What's all this about a grand jury?"

"We want to know where he was when his wife was murdered. Your client has a history of wife abuse . . ."

"I'd be careful what I say, Mr. Carella . . ."

"Yes, sir, I *am* being careful. The police were called to this apartment on two separate occasions, I've already verified that. On the first occasion Mrs. Esposito's eyes were bruised and discolored—that was on August eighteenth, Mr. Lieberman—and on the second occasion she was bleeding from the nose, and the patrolman making the report stated that the nose was broken. That was on November twelfth, last month. With such a record, I feel it's reasonable for us to want to know where your client was at the time of the murder. If he refuses to answer our questions . . ."

"Have you advised him of his rights, Mr. Carella?"

"We're not obliged to. This is still a field investigation; your client's not in custody."

"Do you plan to *take* him in custody?"

"On what grounds, counselor?"

"You tell me. You're the one with all the answers."

"Counselor, let's quit playing games, okay? If your client had nothing to do with his wife's murder, he's got nothing to worry about. But if he refuses to answer our questions, we'll subpoena him to appear before a grand jury, and maybe he'll agree to tell *them* where he was at the time of the murder. Because if he refuses to tell them, as I'm sure you know, he'll be held in contempt. Now we can do whatever you say, Mr. Lieberman. This is Christmas Eve, and you know as well as I that we won't be able to get any grand jury action until the twenty-sixth, but if that's what you want us to do, just say so. If you'd like my advice . . ."

"Oh, are you an attorney, Mr. Carella?"

"No, Mr. Lieberman, are *you?* We want some answers from your client, that's all. My advice is for *you* to advise him to cooperate. That's my advice. Free of charge."

"And worth every penny you're charging," Lieberman said. "Put him back on."

Carella handed the phone to Esposito. "Yeah," he said, and listened. "Uh-huh . . . Are you sure it's okay? . . . All right, I'm sorry to bother you this way, Jerry. Thank you. And Merry Christmas," he said, and hung up. "What are your questions?" he asked Carella.

"Where were you Thursday night between six and seven P.M.?"

"Coming home from work."

"Where's that?" Hawes asked.

"Techno-Systems, Inc., on Rigby and Franchise."

"What do you do there?" Carella asked.

"I'm a computer programmer."

"What time did you leave the office on Thursday?"

"Five-thirty."

"How do you normally get home?"

"By subway."

"It shouldn't have taken you more than a half hour from Rigby and Franchise. If you left the office at five-thirty . . ."

"I stopped for a drink."

"Where?"

"A place called Elmer's, around the corner from the office."

"How long were you there?"

"About an hour."

"Then, actually, you didn't start home till about *six*-thirty, is that it?"

"Six-thirty, a quarter to seven."

"Who were you drinking with, Mr. Esposito?"

"I was alone."

"Are you a regular at Elmer's?"

"I stop in there every now and then."

"Where'd you drink? At a table or at the bar?"

"The bar."

"Does the bartender know you?"

"Not by name."

"Anybody there know you by name?"

"One of the waitresses does. But she wasn't working on Thursday."

"What time did you get back here to Harborview?"

"Seven-thirty or thereabouts. The trains were running slow."

"What'd you do when you got here?"

"There were policemen all over the place. I asked Jimmy what was going on and . . . that was when he told me my wife had been killed."

"By Jimmy, do you mean . . . ?"

"Jimmy Karlson, the security guard."

"What'd you do then?"

"I tried to find out where they'd taken her. They'd moved her body by then. I tried to find out where she was. Nobody seemed to know. I came upstairs and called the police. I had to make six calls before anyone gave me any information."

"Did you know there'd been another murder in the building?"

"Yes, Jimmy told me."

"Told you it was Gregory Craig on the third floor?"

"Yes."

"Did you know Mr. Craig?"

"No."

"Never ran across him in the elevator or anything?"

"I wouldn't have known him if I'd seen him."

"What'd you do when you found out where they'd taken your wife?"

"I went to the morgue and made a positive identification."

"To whom?"

"I don't know who it was. One of the medical examiners, I guess."

"What time was that?"

"Around nine o'clock. They said I ... I could have the body at noon Friday. So I came back here and called the funeral parlor and made arrangements to ... to have her picked up."

"Mr. Esposito," Carella said, "we'll have to check with Elmer's to make sure you were there. It would help us if we had a photograph we could show the bartender. Would you happen to have a recent picture?"

"My attorney didn't say I could give you a picture."

"Call him again if you like," Carella said. "That's the only thing we'll use it for, to show at Elmer's for identification."

"I guess that's okay," Esposito said. He started out of the room, turned, and said, "I didn't kill her. We had our troubles, but I didn't kill her."

They did not get to Elmer's till almost 7:00 P.M.

The bar on Christmas Eve was packed with men and women who had no place else to go, no cozy hearths, no glowing Christmas trees, only the dubious comfort of each other's company. They lined the bar and sat at the tables, and raised their glasses in yuletide toasts, and watched the television set, on which a movie about a family holiday reunion was showing. There were two bartenders behind the bar. Neither of them had been working on Thursday night, when Esposito claimed to have been drinking here alone for an hour or more. They recognized his picture, but they couldn't say he'd been here since they themselves hadn't been here. The bartender who'd been working on Thursday—they explained that only one man worked the bar during the week and two on weekends—was a man named Terry Brogan, who was a moonlighting city fireman. They gave the detectives Brogan's home number and also the number at Engine Company Number Six, uptown in one of the city's highest fire-rate districts. From the phone booth in the bar they called Brogan at home and got no answer. They called the firehouse and spoke to a captain named Ronnie Grange, who said Brogan had taken his wife and kids to Virginia for the Christmas holidays; his sister lived in Virginia.

When they left the bar, Carella said, "I'll tell you one thing, Cotton."

"What's that?"

"Don't ever get murdered just before Christmas."

They shook hands on the sidewalk, wished each other a

70

Merry Christmas, and then walked off in opposite directions toward the two different subway lines that would take them home.

It was beginning to snow again.

Carella did not get home that night till almost eight-thirty. The snow was raising hell with the subway system on its aboveground tracks, and the trains were infrequent and plodding. Outside the Riverhead house he struggled his way through snowdrifts to the front door. There was a kid up the street who was supposed to shovel the walks everytime it snowed. They paid him $3 an hour for the job, but it was obvious he hadn't been here since yesterday's storm. The new storm had tapered off a bit; the air was bristling with the tiniest of crystals. He stamped his feet on the front porch. The wreath on the door was hanging a bit askew; he straightened it and then opened the door and went inside.

The house had never looked more welcoming. A roaring blaze was going in the fireplace, and the tree in the corner of the room was aglow with reds, yellows, blues, greens, and whites that reflected in the hanging ornaments. Teddy was wearing a long red robe, her black hair pulled to the back of her head in a ponytail. She came to him at once and hugged him before he had taken off his coat. He remembered again the afternoon before; he would have to tell her that Hillary Scott had tried to amputate his lower lip with her teeth.

He had mixed himself a martini and was sitting in the chair near the fire when the twins came into the living room. Both were in pajamas and robes. April climbed into his lap; Mark sat at his feet.

"So," Carella said, "you finally got to see Santa."

"Uh-huh," April said.

"Did you tell him all the things you want?"

"Uh-huh," April said.

"Dad . . ." Mark said.

"We missed you a lot," April said quickly.

"Well, I missed you, too, darling."

"Dad . . ."

"Don't tell him," April said.

"He's got to know sooner or later," Mark said.

"No, he don't."

"Doesn't."

"I *said* doesn't."

"You *said* don't."

"Anyway, don't tell him."

71

"Don't tell me what?" Carella asked.

"Dad," Mark said, avoiding his father's eyes, "there is no such thing as Santa Claus."

"You told him," April said, and glared at her brother.

"No such thing, huh?" Carella said.

"No such thing," Mark repeated, and returned April's glare.

"How do you know?"

"Cause there's hundreds of them all over the street," Mark said, "and nobody can move that fast."

"They're his helpers," April said. "Isn't that right, Dad? They're all his helpers."

"No, they're just these guys," Mark said.

"How long have you known this?" Carella asked.

"Well . . ." April said, and cuddled closer to him.

"How long?"

"Since last year," she said in a tiny voice.

"But if you *knew* there wasn't any Santa, why'd you agree to go see him?"

"We didn't want to hurt your feelings," April said, and again glared at her brother. "Now you hurt his feelings," she said.

"No, no," Carella said. "No, I'm glad you told me."

"It's you and Mommy who's Santa," April said, and hugged him tight.

"In which case, you'd better get to bed so we can feed the reindeer."

"What reindeer?" she asked, her eyes opening wide.

"The whole crowd," Carella said. "Donder and Blitzen and Dopey and Doc . . ."

"That's Snow *White!*" April said, and giggled.

"Is it?" he said, grinning. "Come on, bedtime. Busy day tomorrow."

He took them to their separate rooms, and tucked them in, and kissed them good-night. As he was leaving Mark's room, Mark said, "Dad?"

"Yes, son?"

"*Did* I hurt your feelings?"

"No."

"Are you sure?"

"Positive."

"Cause . . . you know . . . I thought it would be better than lying."

"It always is," Carella said, and touched his son's hair, and oddly felt like weeping. "Merry Christmas, son," he said

72

quickly, and turned from the bed, and snapped out the light.

Teddy came out of the kitchen with a tray of hot cheese puffs and then went to say her own good-nights to the children. When she came back into the living room, Carella was mixing himself a second martini. She cautioned him to go easy.

"Long, hard day, honey," he said. "Do you want one of these?"

A scotch, please, she said. *Very light.*

"Where's Fanny?" he asked.

In her room, wrapping gifts.

They sat before the fire, sipping their drinks, nibbling at the cheese puffs. She told him dinner would be ready in a half hour or so; she hadn't been sure what time he'd be getting home; it was heating in the oven now. He apologized for not having called, but he and Hawes had been on the go since early this morning, and he simply hadn't found a spare moment. She asked him how the case was going, and he told her all about Hillary Scott and her twin sister, Denise, told her how Hillary had known not only Teddy's first name but her maiden name as well, told her she'd somehow divined April's name, told her she'd known that April resembled her mother.

Then he told her about the kiss.

Teddy listened.

He told her how he'd tried to pull away from Hillary, told her she'd fastened to his mouth like an embalmer's trocar trying to drain his fluids, told her all about the trance that had followed, Hillary shaking and swaying and talking in a spooky voice about drowning and somebody hearing something, somebody stealing something. Teddy listened and said nothing. She remained uncommunicative all through dinner, her hands busy with her utensils, her eyes avoiding his. After dinner they carried the wrapped presents up from where they'd hidden them in the basement and arranged them under the tree. He told her he'd better shovel the walks before the snow froze solid, and she remembered then to tell him that the boy up the street had phoned Fanny earlier to say he wouldn't be able to get to the house over the weekend because he had to go to his grandmother's.

Outside, shoveling snow, Carella wondered if he should have told Teddy about the kiss after all. He had not mentioned that Hillary Scott looked like a younger version of her, and he was glad now that he hadn't. The air had turned very cold. When he came back into the house, he stood before the dwindling fire for several moments, warming himself, and then went into the bedroom. The light was out. Teddy was in bed. He undressed silently and got into bed with her. She lay stiffly beside him; her breathing told him she was still awake. He snapped on the light.

"Honey, what is it?" he said.

You kissed another woman, she said.

"No, *she* kissed me."

That's the same thing...

"And besides, it wasn't a kiss. It was ... I don't know *what* the hell it was."

It was a kiss; that's what the hell it was, Teddy said.

"Honey," he said, "believe me, I ..."

She shook her head.

"Honey, I *love* you. I wouldn't kiss Jane *Fonda* if I found her wrapped under the Christmas tree tomorrow morning." He smiled and then said, "And you know how I feel about Jane Fonda."

Oh? Teddy said. *And how* do *you feel about Jane Fonda?*

"I think she's ... well, she's a very attractive woman," Carella said, and had the feeling he was plowing himself deeper than any of the snowdrifts outside. "The point I'm trying to make ..."

I once dreamed Robert Redford was making love to me, Teddy said.

"How was it?" Carella asked.

Pretty good, as a matter of fact.

"Honey?" he said.

She watched his lips.

"I love you to death," he said.

Then no more kisses, she said, and nodded. *Or I'll break your goddamn head.*

6

The Mayor, when asked by reporters how he planned to get the streets clear before the heavy holiday traffic began, said with customary wit and style, "Boys, this is nothing but a simple snow job." The members of the press did not find his remark amusing. Neither did the cops of the Eighty-seventh.

Those who were unlucky enough to have caught the midnight to 8:00 A.M. shift on Christmas Day worked clear through to ten in the morning, by which time the relieving detectives began arriving at the squadroom in dribs and drabs. There were eighteen detectives attached to the Eighty-seventh Squad, and they divided among them the three shifts that constituted their working day, six men to each shift. The 8:00 A.M. to 4:00 P.M. shift (or—as it turned out—the 10:00 A.M. to 6:00 P.M.) was shared by Meyer Meyer, Hal Willis, Bob O'Brien, Lou Moscowitz, Artie Brown, and a transfer from the Two-One named Pee Wee Wizonski. Wizonski was six feet four inches tall, weighed 208 pounds in his underwear and socks, and suffered a great many slings and arrows about being Polish. There was not a day that went by without someone in the squadroom telling another Polish joke. On Christmas Day (which was Wizonski's holiday), Lou Moscowitz (who was celebrating Chanukah) told about Pope John Paul II's first miracle: He changed wine into water. Wizonski did not think the joke was funny. Nobody, including the Mayor, was having much luck with his jokes today.

The fireworks started at about ten-thirty.

They started with a so-called "family dispute" on Mason and Sixth. Not too many years ago Mason Avenue had been known far and wide as *la l'ia de Putas*—Whore Street. The hookers along that seedy stretch of Puerto Rican turf had since left it for greener pastures downtown, where they could turn a trick in a massage parlor for a quick forty to eighty dollars, depending on the services rendered. *La l'ia de Putas* was now simply *la l'ia*—the Street—a combination of pool parlors, porno bookshops, porn-flick theaters, greasy spoons, Mom and Pop groceries, a dozen or more bars, and a storefront church dedicated to saving the souls of those who frequented the area. Except for the church—which squatted in one-story religious hopefulness between the grimy buildings sandwiching it—the classy emporiums lining the Street were on the ground floors of tenements that housed people who were willing to settle for grubby surroundings in return for some of the cheapest rents to be found anywhere in the city. It was in one of these apartments that the family dispute took place.

The two patrolmen responding to the call were confronted with a distinctly unholidaylike scene. There were a pair of bodies in the living room, both of them wearing nightgowns, both of them the victims of a shooting. One of them, a woman, was sitting dead in a chair near the telephone, the receiver still clutched in her bloody hand. It was she, they later learned, who had placed the call to Emergency 911. The second victim was a sixteen-year-old girl, sprawled face downward on the patched linoleum, similarly dead. The woman who'd placed the call to 911 had said only, "Send the police; my husband is going crazy." The patrolmen had expected a family dispute, but not one of such proportions. They had knocked on the apartment door, received no answer, tried the knob, and then entered somewhat casually —this was Christmas Day; this was Chanukah. Now they both drew their pistols and fanned out into the room. A closed door was at one end of it. The first patrolman—a black cop named Jake Parsons—knocked on the door and was greeted with an immediate fusillade of shots that ripped huge chunks out of the wood paneling and would have done the same to his head if he hadn't thrown himself flat to the floor in instant reflex. Both cops backed out of the apartment.

On the radio in the car downstairs, they reported to Desk Sergeant Murchison that it looked like they had a double homicide here, not to mention somebody with a gun behind a locked door. Murchison called upstairs to the squadroom. Pee Wee Wizonski, who was catching, took his holster and pistol from the drawer of his desk, motioned to Hal Willis across the room, and was out through the gate in the railing even before Willis put on his coat. Murchison downstairs put a call through to Homicide and also to the Emergency Squad covering this section of the city. If there was a guy with a gun behind a locked door, this was a job for the volunteer Emergency cops, and not mere mortals. The Emergency cops were already there when Wizonski and Willis made the scene. Together the detectives from the Eight-Seven looked a lot like

76

Mutt and Jeff or Laurel and Hardy. Wizonski was the biggest detective on the squad; Willis was the smallest, having just barely passed the Police Department's five-foot-eight height requirement. The r.m.p. patrolmen filled them in on what had happened upstairs, and they all went up to the fourth floor again. The Emergency cops, wearing bulletproof vests, went in first. Whoever was behind the locked door fired the moment he heard sounds in the apartment, so they abandoned all notions of kicking in the door. In the corridor outside the assembled cops held a high-level conference.

The two Homicide men assigned to the case were named Phelps and Forbes. They looked a lot like Monoghan and Monroe, who were home just then, opening Christmas gifts. (The men of the Eight-Seven would later learn that Monoghan's wife had presented him with a gold-plated revolver; Monroe's wife had given him a video cassette home recorder upon which he could secretly play the porn tapes he picked up hither and yon in the city.) Phelps and Forbes were disgruntled about having to work on Christmas Day. Phelps was particularly annoyed because he hated Puerto Ricans, and was fond of repeating that if they'd all go back to that goddamn shitty island they'd come from, there'd be no more crime in this city. So here was a Puerto Rican family causing trouble on Christmas Day—assuming the bedbug behind the locked door was indeed Hispanic. "Hispanic" was the word the cops in this city used for anyone of even mildly Spanish descent, except for Phelps and many cops like him who still called them "spics." Even the Deputy Mayor, who'd been born in Mayagüez, was a spic to Phelps.

"We go near that door," Phelps said, "that spic in there'll blow our fuckin heads off."

"Think we can hit the window?" one of the Emergency cops asked.

"What floor is this?" the other one said.

"The fourth."

"How many in the building?"

"Five."

"Worth trying a rope from the roof, don't you think?"

"You guys keep him busy outside the door," the first Emergency cop said. "One of us'll come in the window behind him."

"When you hear us yell," the second Emergency cop said, "kick in the door. We'll get him both ways."

The patrolmen who were first at the scene had meanwhile talked to a lady in an apartment down the hall, who told them there were two daughters in the family—the sixteen-year-old they'd found dead on the floor and a ten-year-old named Consuela. They reported this to the cops working out their strategy in the hallway, and all of them agreed they had what was known as a "hostage situation" here, which made it a bit risky to come flying in the window like Batman. The two Emergency cops were in favor of trying it, anyway, without asking for help from the Hostage Unit. But Phelps and Forbes vetoed them and asked one of the patrolmen to go downstairs and call in for a hostage team. Nobody yet knew whether ten-year-old Consuela was indeed behind that locked door with whoever was shooting the gun or out taking a stroll in the snow instead.

A genuine hostage situation normally brought a lot of muckamucks to the scene, even if the scene happened to be in a Puerto Rican section of town. By eleven o'clock that morning, when the two Hostage Unit cops arrived, there were four sergeants, a lieutenant, and a captain standing in the crowded hallway with all the others. The captain was in charge of the operation now, and he laid his plans like someone about to storm the Kremlin, telling the Emergency cops he did indeed want a man on a rope from the roof coming down to the window while the Hostage cops talked to the guy through the door. He wanted bulletproof vests on everybody, including the man coming down on the rope. He wanted Wizonski and Willis in vests as backups behind the Hostage cops at the door. The Emergency cop who planned to make the descent from the roof told him the vest weighed a ton and a half, and he'd have trouble enough on the rope with this wind, never mind wearing a vest that might send him plummeting to the street four stories below. The captain insisted on the vest. They all were ready to take up their positions when the door opened and a thin guy wearing only undershorts threw an empty Colt .45 automatic out into the living room and came out with his hands up over his head. He was weeping. His ten-year-old daughter, Consuela, was on the bed behind him. He had smothered her with a pillow. The captain seemed disappointed that he would not now have the opportunity to put his brilliant plan into action.

Meanwhile, back at the ranch, Meyer Meyer and Bob O'Brien caught a somewhat more elevated squeal. Ordinarily Meyer did not enjoy working with O'Brien. This had nothing to do with O'Brien's personality, skill, or courage. It had to do only with O'Brien's peculiar penchant for getting into situations where it became necessary for him to shoot somebody. O'Brien did not enjoy shooting people. In fact, he went to enormous lengths to avoid having to draw his pistol. But people eager to get shot seemed naturally to gravitate toward him. As a result, because cops don't like to get shot any more than civilians do, and because working with O'Brien increased the possibility that there would be an exchange of unwanted gunfire, most of the cops on the Eighty-seventh tried to arrange it so that they were not too often partnered with him. O'Brien, perhaps wrongly, had been dubbed a hard-luck cop. He himself believed that if anywhere in this city there was a man or woman with a weapon, that weapon would somehow be used against him, and he would have to defend himself. He once told this to the girl he was engaged to marry; she broke the engagement the following week, small wonder.

Today, though—being Christmas and Chanukah both—Meyer felt the possibilities for violence in the company of O'Brien were perhaps tilted eighty-twenty in their favor. The odds soared to ninety-ten when they caught the Smoke Rise squeal. Smoke Rise was the most elegant community within the boundaries of the Eight-Seven, almost a township unto itself, with houses ranging in the $200,000 to $300,000 class, most of them commanding splendid views of the River Harb. Moreover, the squeal was a 10-21—a "Burglary Past"—which meant the thief had done his song and dance and then got off the stage to less than tumultuous applause. There was no danger of anyone's shooting at O'Brien—or of O'Brien shooting back—because the man was nowhere on the premises when they arrived.

Many of the streets in Smoke Rise were named regally—Victoria Circle, Elizabeth Lane, Albert Way, Henry Drive—giving the community a royal tone it neither needed nor desired. The builder, however, taking no chances that *this* area might be confused with some of the seedier sections on this side of town, had named the streets himself when subdividing the tract. When he ran out of Normandys, Plantaganets, Lancasters, Yorks, Tudors, Oranges, and Hanovers, he switched over to Windsors. And when he ran out of royalty, he hit upon names like Westminster and Salisbury and Winchester (which he abandoned because it sounded too much like a rifle) and Stonehenge. The entire place had an absolutely British tone to it. Many of the houses even looked as if they'd have been right at home on some moor in Cornwall.

The burglary had taken place on Coronation Drive, just

around the corner from Buckingham Way. The house was a multigabled, multiturreted stone and leaded-glass wonder that rose on the bank of the river like the queen's summer palace. The man who lived inside the house had earned his fortune as a junk dealer when it was still possible to amass great deals of cash without having to give 70 percent of it to Uncle. He still spoke with a distinct Calm's Point accent, his "deses" and "doses" falling like blasphemies in the vaulted living room with its cathedral ceiling. His family—a wife and two sons—were dressed in their holiday finery. They had left the house at a quarter to eleven, to deliver some Christmas gifts up the street, and had arrived home at twelve-thirty to find the place ransacked. They had called the police at once.

"What'd he take, Mr. Feinberg?" Meyer asked.

"Everything," Feinberg said. "He musta backed a truck in the driveway. The stereo's gone, and the TV, and my wife's furs and jewelry, and all my cameras from the upstairs closet. Not to mention all the presents that were under the tree. Son of a bitch took everything."

In one corner of the living room was a mammoth Christmas tree that must have taken a crew of four to erect and decorate. Meyer did not find the tree strange in a Jewish home. He had struggled with the concept of celebrating Christmas together with the Gentiles ever since his own children were born and had finally succumbed when they were respectively nine, eight, and six. His first compromise had been a wooden orange crate decorated with crepe paper to resemble a chimney. From there he had progressed to a small live spruce complete with a burlapped ball of earth, which he told the children was a Chanukah bush. He had strained his back planting the damn tree in the backyard after Christmas and the very next year had bought a chopped-down pine from the charitable organization selling them in the empty lot on the corner. He did not feel any less Jewish for having a decorated Christmas tree in his home. As with many Gentiles, the holiday for him was one of spirit rather than religion. If anything on earth could bring people together for the briefest tick of time, Meyer was all for it.

Some of his Jewish friends told him he was a closet goy. He told them he was also a closet Jew. It was Meyer's belief that Israel was not the homeland, but a foreign country. He was dedicated to the concept that Israel must survive and, in fact, endure—but there was never any question in his mind that he was first an American, next a Jew, and never an

Israeli. He knew that Israel had accepted within its besieged boundaries homeless Jews from all over the world—but he never forgot that America was accepting homeless Jews long before Israel was even a dream. So yes, he had given money to plant trees in Israel. And yes, he hated with all the passion in his soul the acts of terrorism against that tiny nation. And yes, he longed to see those biblical places he knew of only from the days of his youth, when he was going to cheder six days a week and was, in fact, the most brilliant Hebrew student in the class. He was pleased that Christmas and Chanukah fell on the same day this year. He suspected in his heart of hearts, anyway, that all religious holidays had been agrarian holidays centuries ago; it was no accident that Easter and Passover came so close together each year and sometimes —as with *this* celebration—fell on exactly the same day. Lou Moscowitz, who was a Detective Second on the squad, told Meyer he was no longer a real Jew. Meyer Meyer was a real Jew with every fiber of his being. He was just his own *kind* of real Jew.

The burglar had indeed done a lovely number in the Feinberg house. As the detectives went through it, itemizing the stolen goods, they discovered that many more items had been taken than Feinberg had originally surmised. The premise that the burglar had backed a truck into the driveway now seemed entirely plausible. He had even stolen the boys' bicycles from the garage and had taken the younger boy's prize collection of *Queen* albums. The loss of the albums seemed to distress the kid more than the loss of his new movie camera, a Christmas gift he had left under the tree after opening it. The family's original outrage at the theft was giving way to a numbed sense of loss that had nothing whatever to do with the value of the goods. Someone had been inside this house. An unwelcome intruder had entered and pillaged, and the most valuable thing he'd stolen was the family's sense of inviolate privacy. Since they lacked any real knowledge of whether the burglar had been armed with either explosives or a deadly weapon, the crime seemed to be Third-Degree Burglary: "Knowingly entering or remaining unlawfully in a building with intent to commit a crime therein." But the Criminal Law language was hardly adequate to define the crime that had been committed against the Feinbergs. They would none of them forget this day as long as they lived. For years to come they would tell about the man who had come into their house on Christmas Day, the

81

same day as Chanukah that year—and of what had happened to the two detectives ten minutes after they left the scene of the crime.

Meyer and O'Brien's attention might not have been captured by the moving van had this not been Christmas Day. The van was parked on a side street some fifteen blocks from the Feinberg house and indeed well outside the stone walls that circumscribed the Smoke Rise development. The left rear tire of the van, the one away from the snowbanked curb, was flat. A man wearing a brown leather jacket and a blue woolen watch cap was changing the tire. A tire iron and a lug wrench were on the partially scraped pavement beside him. When they saw the van, neither Meyer nor O'Brien said a word to each other about a moving company working on Christmas Day. They had no need to. Meyer, who was driving, pulled the unmarked sedan into the curb behind the van. Both men got out of the car, one from each side of it. The pavement was still slippery with patches of hardened snow the plows had missed. Their breaths feathered from their mouths as they approached the man lifting the spare tire into place.

"Need any help?" Meyer asked.

"No, I'm fine," the man said. He was in his late twenties, Meyer guessed, a white man with a rather pale complexion that seemed almost chalky against the darkness of his eyes and the black mustache under his nose. The lettering on the side of the truck read CULBERTSON MOVING AND TRUCKING COMPANY. The license plate was a commercial plate from the next state.

"Got you working on Christmas Day, huh?" O'Brien said casually.

"Yeah, you know how it is," the man said.

"Must be an important load," Meyer said. "Sent you to pick it up on Christmas."

"Listen, what's it to you?" the man said. "I got a flat here; I'm trying to change it; why don't you just fuck off, huh?"

"Police officers," O'Brien said, and was reaching into his pocket for his shield when the pistol appeared in the man's hand. The move took them both by surprise. Not many crib burglars—as house and apartment burglars were called—carried weapons. The man committing a burglary at night, especially in a residence where there was a human being at the time, ran the risk of the heaviest burglary rap and might well be armed, even if the gun charge would lengthen his stay in prison. If they'd expected any show of violence—and they

82

truly hadn't—it might have come by way of a sudden grab for the tire iron on the pavement. But the man reached under his jacket, instead, and the gun appeared in his hand, a .38-caliber pistol pulled from the waistband of his trousers and aimed directly at Meyer now.

The gun went off before Meyer could react and draw his own pistol. The man fired twice, both shots taking Meyer in the leg and knocking him to the pavement. O'Brien's gun was in his hand at once. He had no time to think that it was happening to him again. He thought only, *My partner is down,* and then he saw the man turning the gun toward him, and he fired instantly, catching him in the shoulder, and then fired again as the man toppled over, the second bullet taking him in the chest. The gun still in his right hand, O'Brien knelt over the wounded man, grabbed for the handcuffs at his belt in a clumsy left-handed pull, and then rolled him over with no concern for the wounds pouring blood and cuffed his hands behind his back. Out of breath, he turned to Meyer, who lay on the street with one leg buckled under him.

"How you doing?" he asked.

"Hurts," Meyer said.

O'Brien went into the car and pulled the radio mike from the dashboard. "This is Eight-Seven-Four," he said, "on Holmsby and North. Police officer down. I need an ambulance."

"Who's this?" the dispatcher said.

"Detective O'Brien."

As if the dispatcher hadn't already guessed.

The nearest hospital to Smoke Rise was Mercy General on North and Platte. There, as a holy crucifix of nuns fluttered about him in the emergency room, an intern slit Meyer's left trouser leg on both sides, looked at the two holes in his leg—one in the thigh, the other just below the kneecap—and phoned upstairs for immediate use of an operating room. The burglar who'd shot Meyer was afforded the same meticulous care—all God's creatures, large and small. By one o'clock that Christmas afternoon both were doing fine in separate rooms on the sixth floor. A patrolman was posted outside the burglar's room, but that was the only difference.

The burglar's name was Michael Addison. In the van he'd stolen from the Culbertson parking lot in the next state, the police found not only the loot from the Feinberg job but also the flotsam and jetsam of several other burglaries he'd committed that day. Addison refused to admit anything. He said he was a sick man, and he wanted a lawyer. He said he was going to sue O'Brien personally and the city corporately for having shot an innocent person trying to change a tire. O'Brien, leaning over his bed, whispered to him that if his partner came out of this a cripple, Addison had better move to China.

Back at the squadroom, Arthur Brown—who was an English literature freak—mentioned to Miscolo in the Clerical Office that the guy had been named absolutely perfectly for a burglar.

"What do you mean?" Miscolo said.

"Addison and Steal," Brown said, and grinned.

"I don't get it," Miscolo said.

"Steal," Brown said. "S-T-E-A-L."

"I still don't get it," Miscolo said. "You want some coffee?"

This was before a team of six men stole an entire city street.

The call came in at ten minutes to five. By then there had been the expected number of actual suicides or suicide attempts—in fact, a bit more than anyone could remember for previous Christmases. By then Lieutenant Byrnes had personally driven out to Meyer's house to break the news to Sarah. Sarah was relieved to learn her husband had only been shot in the leg; the moment she saw Byrnes on her doorstep she'd assumed the worst of her fears had been realized. Byrnes drove her to the hospital after his brief visit, and she spent the rest of the afternoon with Meyer, who complained that when a man got shot, his wife should bring him a nize bowl tschicken soup. Along about then, as she was holding Meyer's hand between both her own and telling him how glad she was that he was still alive, a truck pulled into Gedney Avenue, and six men got out of it to begin tearing up the cobblestoned street.

Gedney was one of the few areas in the city that still boasted cobblestone streets—or at least until that Christmas Day it did. The cobblestones, some said, went back to when the Dutch still governed the city. Others maintained that the Dutch wouldn't have known a cobblestone from a tulip, and it was the British who'd first paved Gedney. The name of the avenue was British, wasn't it? So it had to be the British. Whoever had paved it, the six men who jumped out of the truck were now unpaving it. The plows had been through Gedney twice already, and the street was relatively clear of snow. The men set to work with great vigor—odd for civil service employees at *any* time, but especially peculiar on Christmas Day—using picks and crowbars, prying loose the

84

precious cobblestones, lifting them into the truck, stacking them row on row there, working with the precision of a demolition squad. All up and down the street, people peered from their windows, watching the men at work, marveling at their dedicated industry. It took the men two hours to unpave the entire block from corner to corner. At the end of that time they piled back into the truck and drove off. No one noticed the license plate of the truck.

But one man was somewhat impressed by the fact that the Department of Public Works—for such it had seemed—was out there doing its bit for this much-maligned city even on Christmas Day. He called the mayor's office to congratulate whoever was manning the phones and got through to someone on the mayor's newly installed Citizens' Hot Line, to whom he poured out his effusive praise. The lady who'd answered the phone suspiciously called the Department of Public Works immediately afterward, got no anwer there, and called the superintendent of the department at home. The superintendent told her there had been no work orders issued to tear up the cobblestones on Gedney Avenue. He suggested that she call the police.

So at five that evening, as the streetlamps came on and the shadows lengthened, Detectives Arthur Brown and Lou Moscowitz stood at one end of the block and looked at the same soil Indians must have trod in their moccasins centuries ago, when Columbus came to this hemisphere to start the whole shebang. Shorn of its cobblestones from end to end, Gedney looked virginal and rustic. Brown and Moscowitz were grinning from ear to ear; even cops appreciated a daring rip-off every now and then.

Carella, at home, felt guilty as hell. Not because someone had carted off a block of cobblestones but because Meyer had been shot twice in the leg. Had Carella switched holidays with him, then maybe Meyer wouldn't have got shot. Maybe Carella would have got shot instead. Thinking about this, he felt a little less guilty. He'd been shot enough times, thanks— once just a few days before Christmas, in fact. But Carella was of Italian descent, and the Italians and Jews in this city shared guilt the way they shared matriarchal families. Carella had a cousin who, if he accidentally drove through a red traffic light, would stop in atonement at the *green* light on the next corner.

So on Christmas night, at eight o'clock, Carella arrived at Mercy Hospital to tell Meyer how guilty he was feeling about not having got shot in Meyer's place. Meyer was feeling guilty himself. It was Meyer's contention that if he hadn't been stupid enough to have got himself shot, then Bob O'Brien wouldn't have been forced into the position of once again having to draw his gun and fire it. Meyer was worried about what this might do to O'Brien's *own* feelings of guilt, even though O'Brien was Irish and consequently less prone.

Carella had brought a pint of whiskey with him. He took it out of his coat pocket, poured a pair of generous shots into two sterile hospital glasses, and together the men drank to the undeniable fact that Meyer was still alive albeit a bit punctured. Carella poured a second pair of drinks, and the men drank to another day dawning tomorrow.

7

The new Lineup Room, or Showup Room as it was alternately called, was in the basement of the station house, adjacent to the holding cells where booked prisoners were kept temporarily, awaiting transportation to the Criminal Courts Building downtown. This provided easy access to live bodies who—if they or their attorneys had no objections—could be paraded before a victim or a witness in the company of the *true* suspect the police hoped would be identified.

In days of yore, a lineup of felony offenders arrested the previous day would be held downtown at Headquarters every morning. The purpose of that bygone lineup was to acquaint detectives from all over the city with the people who were committing crimes here. Detectives attended lineups as often as they attended court. But whereas court appearances were necessary if convictions were to be had, somebody upstairs decided that the daily lineups were a drain on manpower and resulted in a minimum amount of future arrests since the people on the stage were headed for confinement anyway, some of them for life. The lineup was now a strictly local affair and conducted solely for the purpose of identification.

The Lineup Room contained a narrow stage with height markers on the wall behind it and a hanging microphone above it. In front of the stage, and separating the stage from three rows of auditorium seats, was a floor-to-ceiling one-way mirror. The one-way mirror was sometimes called a two-way mirror by cops, but cops rarely agreed on anything except whose day off it was. One-way or two-way, it presented to the people lined up on the stage behind it only their own reflections. On the other side, the people sitting in the auditorium seats could look through what appeared to be a plate glass window for an unobstructed, unobserved view of the men or women lined up beyond.

The lineup that Tuesday morning, December 26, was being held for the express purpose of eliciting from Jerry Mandel a positive identification of Daniel Corbett. Carella had called Mandel at home first thing in the morning and was delighted to learn that the Harborview security guard had returned

87

from his skiing trip without any broken bones. He had set up a time for the lineup and then had called Corbett first at home and then at Harlow House to ask if he would cooperate with the police in this matter. Corbett said he had nothing to hide—he had definitely not been the man who'd announced himself at Harborview on the night Craig was killed.

From the holding cells next door the detectives had selected half a dozen men roughly resembling Corbett—all of them with black hair and brown eyes. From the squadroom upstairs, they recruited Detectives Richard Genero and Jerry Barker, similarly hued. The prisoners, all wearing what they'd had on when arrested, presented a sartorial mix of sweaters, sports jackets; and—in the case of one gentleman pickpocket—a dapper pin-striped suit. Genero and Barker were wearing sports jackets. Daniel Corbett, who'd come to the precinct directly from Harlow House, was wearing a dark blue suit, a paler blue shirt, and a gold-and-blue silk rep tie. As the guest of honor he was allowed to choose his own position in the line. He elected to take the position fourth from the left. When all nine men had silently taken their places behind the one-way mirror, the spotlights went on over the stage. The auditorium beyond remained dark. Carella and Hawes were sitting together with Mandel in the second row center, flanking him.

"Recognize anybody?" Carella said.

"No, not yet," Mandel said. He was, surprisingly for a skier, a chubby little man in his mid-fifties. He had told Carella, before the lineup, that he used to be a professional wrestler. Carella could not possibly imagine him throwing a hammerlock on anyone. Mandel kept staring at the men behind the plate glass.

"Can I eliminate the ones it definitely *wasn't?*" he asked.

"Go right ahead."

"Well, it wasn't the ones on either end there, and it wasn't the one in the middle."

"Frank," Carella said into the microphone on the stand before him, "you can take away Numbers One, Five, and Nine." Genero was standing first in line; he slouched off the stage, looking oddly disappointed that he hadn't been chosen the winner. The other two disqualified men were prisoners from the holding cells. In rapid sequence, Mandel eliminated two more of the prisoners and Detective Barker. There were now three men standing on the stage: the two remaining prisoners and Daniel Corbett.

"Could they say something for me?" Mandel whispered.

"Sure," Carella said. "Gentlemen, would you mind saying in your normal voices, 'I'm Daniel Corbett. I'd like to see Mr. Craig, please.' Number Four, we'll start with you."

Number Four was Daniel Corbett. He cleared his throat and said, "I'm Daniel Corbett. I'd like to see Mr. Craig, please."

"All right, Number Six," Carella said.

Number Six said, "I'm Daniel Corbett. I'd like to see Mr. Craig, please."

"And Number Eight."

Number Eight said, "I'm Daniel Corbett. I'd like to see Mr. Craig, please."

"What do you think?" Carella asked.

"I can't be certain . . ." Mandel said, and paused, "but I think it's the one on the right. Number Eight."

Number Eight was a man named Anthony Ruggiero, who had been arrested early that morning for attempting to break down the door of an apartment just off Grover Avenue, three blocks from the police station. He was drunk at the time, and he claimed he thought it was his own apartment and that the woman who kept telling him to go away was his wife. Carella looked at Hawes, briefly and bleakly, and then thanked Mandel. He went behind the one-way mirror a moment later, like a stage-door Johnny without flowers, and apologized to Corbett for having taken so much of his time.

"So who the hell *was* it?" Carella asked Hawes.

"Somebody Craig knew, that's for sure."

"Had to be. Otherwise, why would he have let him into the apartment? And why would he have had a drink with him?"

"That's right, the autopsy . . ."

"Right, he'd been drinking. In fact, he was *drunk*. But the lab techs couldn't find alcohol traces in any of the glasses."

"Which means they were washed afterwards."

"Which doesn't mean a thing if Craig was drinking alone. But Hillary told me he never drank while he was working. Never. We *know* he was working that afternoon because there was a sheet of paper in the typewriter. And the sentence just trailed off, which makes it reasonable to believe he was interrupted—probably when the killer rang the doorbell. But he let him *in*, Cotton! He knew it wasn't Corbett, and he let him in anyway. And if he never drank while he was working, then he had to have started drinking after he *quit* working. Which means he sat down to have a drink with the man who murdered him."

The two detectives looked at each other.

"What do you think?" Hawes asked.

"I don't know *what* the hell to think. Maybe Craig thought it was just a friendly little visit, have a drink, make yourself comfortable, and out comes the knife."

"It's the knife that bothers me," Hawes said. "The fact that he brought the knife with him."

"Sure, that makes it premeditated."

"Murder One, pure and simple."

"Then why'd he accept a drink first?"

"And what did they talk about between five o'clock and whenever it was he began hacking away?"

The detectives looked at each other again.

"Esposito?" Hawes asked.

"Maybe," Carella said. "He lived in the building; he could have presented himself as the member of some tenants' committee or . . ."

"Then who was it downstairs?"

"What do you mean?"

"Who announced himself as Corbett? That couldn't have been Esposito."

"No," Carella said. "Shit, let's go talk to the Fire Department."

At Engine Company Number Six, a half hour later, they spoke to Terry Brogan, the moonlighting bartender. Brogan looked at the photograph of Warren Esposito, nodded, and said, "Yeah, I know him."

"Was he in Elmer's Thursday night?" Carella asked.

"What was Thursday? The twenty-second?"

"The twenty-first."

"Yeah. Yeah, I was working the bar that night."

"Did Esposito come in?"

"Is that his name?"

"Warren Esposito, yes. Did he . . . ?"

"Serve a guy drinks for months on end, never get to know his name," Brogan said, and shook his head wonderingly.

"Was he there Thursday night?"

"Thursday night, Thursday night," Brogan said, "let me see, what happened Thursday night?" He was thoughtful for several moments. From the second floor of the firehouse, spilling down through the hole surrounding the brass pole, Carella heard a voice saying, "Full boat, kings over." Someone else said, "You've got a fuckin horseshoe up your ass.'"

"I think Thursday was the night the redhead took off her blouse," Brogan said.

"When was that? What time?"

"Musta been about six o'clock," Brogan said. "She came in bombed, and she had three more drinks in an hour. Yeah, it musta been about six. What it was, some guy sitting at the bar said she had to be wearing falsies, tits like that. So she took off the blouse to show him she wasn't."

"Was Esposito there?" Carella said patiently.

"He coulda been. With all that excitement . . . I mean, who was looking anyplace but the redhead's chest?"

"What time did you start work last Thursday?" Hawes said, figuring he'd come in by the side door.

"Four-thirty."

"Esposito told us he was there at five-thirty."

"He coulda been."

"What time did the redhead come in?"

"An hour before she took off her blouse."

"That would've been five o'clock, right?"

"Yeah, about five."

"Okay, were you the only one tending bar at five o'clock?"

"Sure."

"So you were serving the redhead."

"Right."

"So between five and six there was no excitement. Nothing to distract you. So can you try to remember whether or not Warren Esposito came in at five-thirty?"

"Look at the picture again," Carella said.

Brogan looked at the picture again. Carella found himself wondering how the man would behave in a four-alarm fire. What would happen if he hacked his way into a blazing bedroom and found a bare-breasted redhead in there? Would he forget his own name? Would he jump to the street six stories below without a net under him? Would he turn his hose on an open window?

"Yeah, that's right," Brogan said.

"What's right?" Carella asked, wondering if he'd stumbled across another psychic.

"Rob Roys. He drinks Rob Roys. I served the redhead a Manhattan, and then the old fart up the bar a gin on the rocks, and then he came in and ordered a Rob Roy."

"Esposito?"

"Yeah, the guy in the picture here."

"What time?"

"Well, if the redhead came in at five . . . yeah, it musta been five-thirty or thereabouts. Like he said."

"What time did he leave?" Carella asked.

91

"That's hard to say," Brogan said. "Because of all the excitement with the redhead."

"Was he there when the redhead took off her blouse?"

"I'm pretty sure he was. Let me think a minute."

Carella watched him while he thought a minute. Carella imagined he was reconstructing the entire exciting event in his mind. In all his years of police work he had never known an alibi to hinge on a redhead's breasts. But the redhead had come in at five and taken off her blouse at six, and they had just established that Esposito was there at about five-thirty. If Carella had wanted to pull teeth for a living, he would've become a dentist. It seemed, though, that they would have to work Brogan's mouth from bicuspid to molar to canine, tooth by tooth, till they got what they were after.

Brogan began counting off imaginary people lined up along the bar, using the forefinger of his left hand. "Abner at the end of the bar, near the juke, scotch and soda. The secretary from Halston, Inc., next to him, vodka tonic. Then your guy here, Rob Roy. Next to him a guy I never saw before, bourbon and water. Then the redhead, Manhattans. And next to her the guy who made the comment about her tits, also who I never saw before, Canadian and soda. So that's who was there at six o'clock, just before she took off the blouse. So, yeah, your guy was still there at six."

"How do you know it was six?" Hawes asked.

"The news was just coming on. On television. We have a television set over the bar. That's what started the whole thing."

"What do you mean?"

"This girl they got doing the six o'clock news. What's her name? I forget her name."

"I don't know her name," Hawes said.

"But you know who I mean, don't you? Her and this guy do the news together. The six o'clock news."

"Well, what *about* her?" Hawes said.

"Somebody said she had great tits, the girl on television and the redhead said they were falsies, and the guy sitting next to the redhead said something about *hers* being falsies, too, and that was when she took off her blouse to prove they weren't." Brogan grinned appreciatively. "Believe me, they were definitely not falsies."

"So Esposito was there at six o'clock when the news came on and the blouse came off," Carella said.

"Right."

"Was he still there at six-thirty?"

"Six-thirty, six-thirty," Brogan said. "Let me think a minute."

Carella looked at Hawes. Hawes let out his breath through his nose.

"The boss came in about ten minutes after six," Brogan said. "He sees the redhead sitting there at the bar starkers from the waist up, he says, 'What the hell's going on here?' He thinks she's a hooker or something, you know? He tells her to get the hell out of there, he don't want hookers lining up at his bar, bringing heat down on the place. Just between us he collects numbers on the side. So, naturally, he don't want some cop coming in there to bust a hooker and accidentally tumbling to the numbers operation." His voice lowered confidentially. "I'm telling you this because we're all civil service employees," he said. "I don't want to cause the guy no trouble."

"All right, so the boss came in at six-ten," Hawes said. "Was Esposito there when the boss came in?"

"Yeah, he joined in the chorus."

"What chorus?"

"Everybody told the boss to shut up and leave the redhead alone."

"Then what?"

"The boss told her to put on her blouse and get out of there before he called the police. He wasn't *really* going to call no police because then he might get the kind of trouble he wasn't looking for; he was just kind of threatening her, you know?"

"Did she put on the blouse?" Carella asked.

"She put on the blouse."

"At ten minutes after six?"

"At a quarter after six."

"Then what?"

"She left. No, wait. First she called the boss a tight-assed son of a bitch. *Then* she left."

"At six-fifteen?"

"Six-fifteen, right."

"Was Esposito still there when she left?"

"He was still there."

"How do you know?"

"He asked me for another Rob Roy, and he also commented that those were the biggest tits he ever saw in his life."

"Good, so now it's six-fifteen," Carella said. "Was he still there at six-thirty?"

"I gave him his tab at six-thirty."

"How do you know it was six-thirty?"

"Because the news was going off."

"Did he leave when you gave him his tab?"

"He paid it first."

"And *then* did he leave?" Hawes asked.

"He left," Brogan said, and nodded.

"At six-thirty?"

"A few minutes after six-thirty, it musta been."

"How do you know it was Esposito who left?"

"He gave me a five-dollar tip. He said the five bucks was for the floor show."

"Why couldn't you remember all this when we *first* asked you!" Hawes said.

"Because everything in life has a beginning, a middle, an end," Brogan said, and shrugged philosophically.

He had, at long last, established Warren Esposito's alibi. The man had been at Elmer's, drinking and watching an impromptu ecdysiastical performance, just about when his wife was being stabbed to death on the sidewalk outside their building.

They were back at the beginning again, and the middle and end seemed nowhere in sight.

At six o'clock that night car Boy Seven of the Twelfth Precinct was dispatched to 1134 Llewlyn Mews to investigate what the caller had described as "screaming and hollering in the apartment." It was a peculiar fact of police nomenclature in this city that precincts like the Eighty-seventh and the Sixty-third were familiarly and respectively called the Eight-Seven and the Six-Three, whereas all precincts from the First to the Twentieth were called by their full and proper designations. There was no One-Six in this city; it was the Sixteenth. Similarly, there was no One-Two; the men who responded to the call in the Quarter that day after Christmas were cops from the Twelfth.

They got out of the r.m.p. car, stepped over the bank of snow at the curb, and gingerly made their way across the slippery sidewalk to a sculpted black wrought-iron fence surrounding a slate courtyard. They opened the gate in the fence and went through a small copse of Australian pines to the bright orange front door of the building. One of the patrolmen lifted the massive brass knocker on the door and let it fall. He repeated the act four times and then tried the knob. The door was locked. There was no sound from within the place now; they assumed at once that they'd be calling in with a 10-90—an "Unfounded." But being conscientious law enforcement officers, they went around the side of the building and through a small garden banked high with snow, and rapped on the back door, and then peered through a window into a kitchen, and then rapped on the door again, and tried the knob. This door was open.

One of the patrolmen stuck his head into the kitchen and yelled, "Police officers. Anybody home?"

There was no answer.

He looked at the other patrolman. The other patrolman shrugged. Tentatively they entered the apartment, somewhat uncertain of their rights, knowing only that they were responding to a call and supposing it was their duty to investigate thoroughly, especially in view of the unlocked back door—which they guessed they could say indicated forced entry, if push came to shove.

In the wood-paneled library they found a dead man wearing a red smoking jacket with a black velvet collar.

The Detective/Second from the Twelfth Squad was a man named Kurt Heidiger, who responded to the homicide alone because his partner was home sick with the flu and because the squadroom was a madhouse today and nobody could be spared to accompany him. He established at a glance that the probable cause of death was multiple stab wounds, and he learned from the neighbor across the mews—the woman who'd placed the Emergency 911 call—that the dead man's name was Daniel Corbett, and that he worked for a publishing firm called Harlow House.

Heidiger was a smart cop and a prodigious reader. When the city's papers weren't on strike, and that was rarely, he read all three of them from first page to last every day of the week. He recalled reading on Friday about the death of a writer named Gregory Craig—whose book *Deadly Shades* he had also read—and he remembered seeing a black-edged *in memoriam* notice on the book page of this morning's edition of the city's more literary newspaper; the notice had been placed by a publisher called Harlow House. Primarily he remembered that Craig had been the victim of a brutal stabbing. There probably was no connection, but Heidiger was too smart and too experienced to allow even the smallest of possibilities to go unexplored. When he was through with all the Medical Examiner-lab technician-Homicide Division bullshit at the scene, he went back to the office and checked with Headquarters for the name of the detective investigating the Craig murder. He called the Eighty-seventh Precinct, was connected with the squadroom upstairs, and was told by a detective named Bert Kling that Carella had gone home at a little after four. He reached Carella in the Riverhead house at a quarter past eight. Carella listened attentively and then told Heidiger he'd meet him at the scene in an hour.

It looked as if they had another companion case.

Jennifer Groat was a tall bony blonde in her late forties, her hair piled haphazardly on top of her head, the front of her long blue robe stained with what looked like either mayonnaise or custard. She explained that she was just getting ready for bed. The holidays had simply *exhausted* her, and now *this* had to happen. She made it plain from the moment she admitted the detectives to her apartment that she was sorry she'd called the police at *all*. In this city, it was best to mind your own business and go your own way.

"When you called nine-eleven," Heidiger said, "you mentioned that you heard screaming and hollering in the Corbett apartment . . ."

"Yes," Jennifer said, and nodded.

"We have the call clocked in at five-fifty-three, is that about right?"

"Yes, it was a little before six."

"What kind of hollering and screaming did you hear?"

"What kinds of hollering and screaming *are* there?" Jennifer said. "Hollering and screaming is hollering and screaming."

"By screaming . . ."

"Somebody screaming at the top of his lungs."

"And by hollering?"

"I don't know what the person was hollering."

"Was he hollering for help?"

"I don't know."

"Was it the same person doing both the hollering *and* the screaming?"

"I don't know. I heard the noise over there, and I called the police. There's *always* noise over there, but this was worse than usual."

"What do you mean?" Carella asked at once. "What kind of noise?"

"Parties all the time. People drinking and laughing at all hours of the night. Well, you know. With the kind of friends Mr. Corbett had . . ." She let the sentence trail.

"What kind of friends were they?" Heidiger asked.

96

"You know."

"No, I'm sorry, we don't."

"Pansies," she said. "Fruits. Faggots. *Gay* people," she said, stressing the word "gay" and pulling a face.

"Homosexuals," Carella said.

"Queers," Jennifer said.

"And they were partying all the time, is that it?"

"Well, not *all* the time. But enough of the time. I'm a telephone operator; I work the midnight shift; I try to catch a little nap before I leave the house each night. With all the noise over there, it's impossible. I was about to take my nap *now,* in fact. If it isn't one thing, it's always another," she said, and again grimaced.

"Those friends of Mr. Corbett's," Carella said, "how do you know they were homosexuals?" He was remembering that Corbett's alibi for his whereabouts at the time of the Craig murder was a married woman named Priscilla Lambeth who had entertained him on her office couch.

"One of them came here just the other night," she said, "looking for the big *party.*" She lisped the word "party" and accompanied it with a mincing limp-wristed gesture. "He didn't realize Mr. Corbett lived on the other side of the mews."

"Did he give you his name?" Heidiger asked.

"Who?"

"The man who came here looking for Corbett."

"Man? Don't make me laugh."

"Did he give you his name?"

"Why would he? He asked for *Danny*"—and again she lisped the word and hung her limp wrist on the air—"and I told him this was eleven-thirty-six, and what he wanted was eleven-thirty-four. He thanked me kindly and went flitting across the courtyard."

"This was when, did you say?"

"Christmas Eve. Mr. Corbett had a big Christmas *Eve* party. *I* had to work on Christmas Eve, *I* was trying to get some sleep. Instead, I got a fruit knocking on the door asking for *Danny.*"

"Did you see anyone entering the courtyard tonight?" Carella asked.

"No, I didn't."

"I mean, before you heard the screaming."

"Nobody. I was in the tub, in fact, when I heard all the fuss. What I like to do is take a bath before dinner. Then I eat a little something, take my nap, which I should be doing now," she said, and glanced at the clock, "and then get dressed and go to work."

"Did you see anybody in the courtyard *after* you heard the screams?"

"I stayed in the tub."

"You mean you didn't immediately call the police?"

"No, I called them when I got out of the tub. There's always noise over there. If I called every time I heard noise, it'd be a full-time job."

"What time was it when you heard the screams?"

"I don't wear a watch in the tub."

"How long did you stay in the tub? After you heard the screams, I mean."

"About fifteen minutes, I guess."

"The call came in at five-fifty-three," Heidiger said. "That means you heard the screams at . . ." He hesitated, doing his mental calculation, and then said, "Approximately twenty to six, somewhere in there."

"I would guess."

"When you got out of the tub," Carella said, "did you see anyone in the courtyard? Anyone near the Corbett apartment?"

"I didn't look. I went to the phone and called the police. I figured if I didn't do something about it, the noise would go on all night. And I wanted to have my dinner and take my nap in peace."

"Was the screaming still going on?"

"No, it had stopped by then."

"But you called the police anyway."

"Who knew when it might start again? You know how those people are," she said.

"Mm," Carella said. "Well, thank you very much, Miss Groat. Sorry to have bothered you."

In the street outside, Heidiger lighted a cigarette, belatedly offered one to Carella, who refused, and then said, "Ever talk to this Corbett guy?"

"Last Saturday," Carella said.

"Strike you as being a fag?"

"Seemed straight as an arrow."

"Who can tell these days, huh?" Heidiger said. "How about Craig?"

"He was living with a beautiful twenty-two-year-old girl."

"Mm," Heidiger said. "So what do you make of it? Any connection here, do you think?"

"I don't know."

"Knife in both murders."

"Yeah."

"If the witch in there was right, this one might've been a lovers' quarrel."

"Maybe. But we've only got her word for what Corbett was. Did she strike you as a particularly reliable character witness?"

"She struck me as a particularly reliable *character*," Heidiger said dryly. "You want a beer or something? Officially I'm still on duty, but fuck it."

"Shooflies are heavy around the holidays," Carella said, smiling.

"Fuck the shooflies, too," Heidiger said. "I've been with the department twenty-two years; I never took a nickel from anybody in all that time. Just *let* them bring charges for a glass of beer; I'd like to see them do that."

"Go on without me," Carella said. "There's somebody I want to talk to."

"Keep in touch," Heidiger said, and shook hands with him, and walked off up the street. In the phone booth on the corner, Carella checked the Isola directory for a Priscilla Lambeth listing, found none under her name, but *two* for a Dr. Howard Lambeth—one for his office and one for his residence. The residential number was Higley 7–8021, which sounded like the number Carella had dialed from Corbett's apartment last Saturday. Ha dialed the number now. A woman answered the phone; her voice sounded familiar.

"Mrs. Lambeth?" Carella said.

"Yes?"

"Priscilla Lambeth?"

"Yes?"

"This is Detective Carella; we talked last Saturday, do you re—"

"I asked you not to call here again," she said.

"Daniel Corbett has been murdered," Carella said. "I'd like to talk to you. I can come there, or we can meet someplace."

There was a long silence on the line.

"Mrs. Lambeth?" he said.

The silence lengthened.

"Which would you prefer?" Carella said.

"I'm thinking." He waited. "Give me half an hour," she said. "I'll be walking the dog in half an hour. Can you meet me on Jefferson and Juniper at . . . what time is it now?"

"Close to ten."

"Make it ten-thirty," she said. "He's a golden retriever."

As befitted an editor of children's books, Priscilla Lambeth was a petite brunette with a pixie face and wide, innocent eyes. There was a huge dog at the end of her leash, a hound intent on racing through the city streets in headlong search of yet another lamppost to sniff, dragging Priscilla willy-nilly behind him. Carella was hard put to keep up.

Priscilla was wearing a dark blue ski parka over blue jeans and boots. She was hatless, and the wind caught at her short dark hair, bristling it about her head and giving her the appearance of someone who'd just been unexpectedly startled out of her wits—rather close to the truth. She told Carella at once that she'd been truly shocked by what he'd revealed on the telephone. She still couldn't get over it. Danny murdered? Incredible! Who would want to kill a sweet, loving person like Danny?

Jefferson Avenue at this hour of the night was largely deserted, the shopwindows shuttered, a fierce wind tossing up eddies of snow from the banks along the curbs. To the north, on Hall Avenue, there were still strollers, still browsers in the bookshops that remained open till midnight in hope of catching the after-theater crowd drifting southward from the Stem and the theatrical district. Even those hardy souls were small in number on a night like this, with the wind howling in over the River Harb and the temperature hovering at twenty-four degrees Farenheit. Carella walked with his hands in his pockets, the collar of his coat pulled high on his neck, his shoulders hunched. The dog trotted ahead of them like the lead dog on a sled team, tugging at the leash, yanking Priscilla behind them and by association Carella as well.

"Mrs. Lambeth," he said, "Daniel Corbett told us you and he had been intimate. The thing I want to . . ."

"I wish you wouldn't say that," Priscilla said. Her voice was tiny, the voice of an eight-year-old trapped in a thirteen-year-old's pubescent body. He wondered briefly what kinds of books she edited. Picture books? Had his daughter, April, read any of the books that crossed Priscilla Lambeth's desk? The dog stopped at another lamppost, sniffed it, found it to his liking, and lifted his hind leg.

"But it's true, isn't it?" Carella said.

"Yes, it's true. It's just that when you put it that way . . ."
The dog was off again, almost yanking her arm out of its

socket. She held gallantly to the leash, out of breath, racing along behind the dog. Carella trotted beside her. His face was raw from the wind; his nose was running. He took a handkerchief from the pocket of his coat, hoped he wasn't coming down with something, and blew his nose.

"Mrs. Lambeth," he said, out of breath himself, "I'm not particularly interested in how you and Daniel Corbett passed the time of day. But he was murdered tonight, and a neighbor intimated . . . look, would you do me a favor, please? Would you tie that dog to a lamppost so we can stand *still* for a minute and talk?"

"He hasn't pooped yet," she said.

Carella looked at her.

"Well, all right," she said.

She yanked her gloves off, tucked them under her arm, and tied the leash around the stanchion of a NO PARKING sign. The dog began howling at once, like Fang, Son of Claw. Carella led her to the sheltered doorway of a men's clothing store, waited while she put on her gloves again, and then said, "Was Daniel Corbett a homosexual?"

She seemed genuinely startled. Her eyes opened wider. They were green, he now noticed. They searched his face as though eager for him to assure her he'd just told a bad joke.

"Was he?" Carella asked.

"He didn't seem to be," she said in the same tiny voice, almost a whisper now.

"Any indication at all that he might have been?"

"I don't know what you mean."

"Mrs. Lambeth, you've been intimate with him for the past month or so, according to what he . . ."

"Yes, but not that often."

"Two or three times, is that right?"

"Well, yes, I suppose."

"What I want to know is if during any of your meetings . . ."

"He performed adequately, if that's what you want to know."

"No, that's *not* what I want to know."

"I find this embarrassing," Priscilla said.

"So did Corbett. But murder is the biggest embarrassment of them all. During any of your meetings did he in any way indicate to you that he might *also* be interested in men?"

"No."

101

"Did he ever bring a man along with him?"

"What do you mean?"

"I'm assuming you met someplace away from the office . . ."

"Yes."

"Was there ever a man with him?"

"Once."

"Who?"

"Alex Harrod."

"Who's that?"

"A paperback editor. At Absalom Books."

"Is he a homosexual?"

"I'm not that familiar with homosexuals."

"Why was he there?"

"Danny thought it would be . . . well . . . he thought we'd be less noticeable if someone else was there with us."

"Where was this?"

"The Hotel Mandalay bar."

"When?"

"Last month sometime."

"What happened at that meeting, can you tell me?"

"Nothing. Alex had a few drinks, and then he left. Danny and I . . . went upstairs to a room he'd booked."

"What'd you talk about?"

"Danny and I?"

"No, the three of you. While you were together in the bar."

"Books. Danny had some books he thought Absalom might want to buy."

"That's all? Books?"

"Yes. Well . . . yes."

"What else, Mrs. Lambeth?"

"Nothing. Not then. Not in the bar."

"Where then?"

"Really, I *do* find this . . ."

"Where, Mrs. Lambeth? In the room? What did you talk about in the room?"

The dog was howling like a hungry wolf waiting for an Eskimo to come out of his igloo. Together the dog and the wind created a veritable Antarctic symphony. Priscilla glanced at the dog and said, "I have to untie him."

"No, you *don't* have to," Carella said. "I want to know what Corbett said to you after that meeting with Harrod."

"It was pillow talk," Priscilla said. "People say things in bed . . ."

"Yes, what did he say?"

"He asked me if I'd . . . if I'd ever had a two-on-one."

"What did you think he meant by that?"

"He meant . . . me and two men."

"Did he have any particular man in mind?"

"He asked me what I thought of Alex Harrod."

"Was that the man he had in mind?"

"I . . . guess so. Yes. He asked me if I found Alex attractive. And he . . . suggested that it might be . . . fun to try it together with him sometime."

"What was your reaction to that?"

"I said I thought Alex was attractive."

Her voice was so low now that he almost could not hear her. The dog and the wind refused to end their collaboration. Carella could do nothing about the wind, but he wanted to shoot the dog.

"Did you agree to such an arrangement?"

"I said I'd . . . think about it."

"Did the suggestion ever come up again?"

There was a long silence, broken only by the howling of the dog and the wind.

"Did it?"

"Yes."

"When?"

"At the Christmas party."

"Corbett again suggested that the three of you . . ."

"Yes."

"And what was your response?"

Priscilla looked at the dog. Her arms were crossed over her breasts, her gloved hands tucked into her armpits. She kept watching the dog.

"What was your response?" Carella said.

"I told him I . . . I might like to try it. We had both had a little too much to drink; this was the annual Christmas party . . ."

"Did you set up a date?"

"Yes, we . . . we did."

"For when?"

"My husband is going to Wisconsin this week. His mother lives in Wisconsin, she's very sick, he's going out there to see her. We planned to . . . to go to Danny's place in the country over the New Year's Eve weekend. My husband won't be back till . . . till the second."

"By the country, do you mean Gracelands?"

"Yes, Danny has a house up there."

103

"Is it his house?"

"I think so."

"Or does he share it with Alex Harrod?"

"I don't know."

"Thank you, Mrs. Lambeth," Carella said. "You can untie the dog now."

The Isola directory listing for Alexander Harrod gave his address as 511 Jacaranda, downtown in the Quarter. Carella called first to say that he was investigating a homicide and wanted to talk to Harrod. He did not mention that the homicide victim was Daniel Corbett; he wanted to save that for the face-to-face. Harrod protested that it was already after eleven and wanted to know if this couldn't wait till morning. Carella went into his long song and dance about the first twenty-four hours in a homicide being most important to the investigating detective and finally prevailed upon Harrod to give him a half hour of his time.

The building in which Harrod lived was a three-story brick walk-up painted white. Carella rang the downstairs bell, got an answering buzz, and climbed the stairs to the third floor. The apartment was at the end of the hall. He knocked on the door, and it opened at once, almost as if Harrod had been impatiently behind it. Carella was surprised to find himself looking into the face of a tall, slender black man. Priscilla had not mentioned to him that the third man in the proposed *ménage à trois* was black.

"Mr. Harrod?" he said.

"Yes, please come in."

He was wearing blue jeans and a tight-fitting white T-shirt under a blue cardigan sweater with a shawl collar. He was barefooted, and he padded now into a living room decorated in what Carella termed "chotchkepotchke," an expression he'd picked up from Meyer. The walls were lined with shelves and shelves of objets d'art and trinkets, small vases with dried flowers, photographs in miniature oval frames, keys picked up in antique shops, the letter *A* in various sizes, some in brass, others of wood painted gold, enough books to fill a good-sized bookstore, little framed notes that were obviously of sentimental value to Harrod. The sofa was done in soft black leather and heaped with pillows of various sizes, some of them mirrored, some of them tasseled, that spilled over onto the floor to form yet another seating area. A painting of two men wrestling was on the wall over the couch. The floor

104

was covered with a white shag rug. The heat was turned up very high; Carella wondered if Harrod grew orchids in his spare time.

"Is this about Gregory Craig?" Harrod asked.

"What makes you think so?"

"I know he was killed, and Absalom published the paperback of *Shades*."

"It's about Daniel Corbett," Carella said.

"Danny? What about him?"

"He was murdered early tonight," Carella said, and watched for Harrod's reaction. The reaction came at once. Harrod backed away a pace, as though Carella had punched him full in the face.

"You're putting me on," he said.

"I wish I were."

"Danny?" he said.

"Daniel Corbett, yes. He was stabbed to death sometime between five-thirty and six o'clock tonight."

"Danny?" Harrod repeated blankly, and suddenly he was weeping. Carella watched him and said nothing. Harrod pulled a tissue from the back pocket of his jeans and dried his eyes. "I'm sorry . . . we . . . we were good friends," he said.

"That's why I'm here, Mr. Harrod," Carella said. "How close was your relationship?"

"I just told you. We were good friends."

"Mr. Harrod, is it true that you and Mr. Corbett planned to go to Gracelands this weekend with a woman named Priscilla Lambeth?"

"Where'd you hear that?" Harrod asked.

"From Mrs. Lambeth."

"Well, then . . ."

"Is it true?"

"Yes, but that doesn't mean . . ."

"Mr. Harrod, are you aware that Daniel Corbett suggested the three of you go to bed together?"

"I was aware of that, yes. It still doesn't mean . . ."

"Wasn't that the purpose of the planned trip to Gracelands?"

"Yes, but . . ."

"Had you and Mr. Corbett ever done this before?"

"No."

"I don't mean with Priscilla Lambeth. I mean with *any* woman."

"What's that got to do with his murder?"

"You haven't answered my question."

"I don't have to answer a damn thing," Harrod said. "Let me ask *you* something, Mr. Detective. If you didn't think I was gay, would you be here asking the same questions?"

"I don't give a damn about your sexual preferences, Mr. Harrod. That's *your* business. I'm here to . . ."

"Sure," Harrod said. "Go tell that to every other cop in this city."

"I'm not every other cop in this city, I'm me. I want to know whether you went along with the idea of sharing a bed with Daniel Corbett and Priscilla Lambeth."

"Why?"

"Were you and Corbett lovers?"

"I don't have to answer that."

"That's true, you don't. Where were you at five-forty tonight, Mr. Harrod?"

"Right here. I came straight from work."

"Where's Absalom Books?"

"Uptown on Jefferson."

"What time did you get here?"

"Five-thirty, little bit after."

"Did you talk to Mr. Corbett at any time today?"

"We spoke, yes."

"What about?"

"Nothing important."

"The trip to Gracelands?"

"The subject may have come up."

"How'd you feel about the trip?"

"Here comes the gay shit again," Harrod said.

"You're the one who keeps bringing it up. How'd you feel about the trip?"

"I didn't want to go, all right?"

"Why not?"

"Because I was . . ." Harrod suddenly clenched his fists. "You have no right to hassle me this way. I was nowhere near Danny's place when he was . . . when he was . . ." He began weeping again. "You son of a bitch," he said, and again pulled the tattered tissue from his pocket and dried his eyes. "You're always hassling us. Can't you, for Christ's sake, leave us *alone?*"

"Tell me about the trip," Carella said.

"I didn't want to go," Harrod said, weeping. "I was sick and tired of . . . of Danny bringing all these fag hags around. He was AC/DC; all right, I could live with that. But these . . . these goddamn *women* he was always intruding into our

106

relationship . . ." He shook his head. "I told him to make up his mind. He . . . he promised this would be the last time. He said I'd enjoy it. He said she found me attractive."

"How'd you find her?"

"Repulsive," Harrod said flatly.

"But you agreed to go."

"For the last time. I told him I'd walk if he kept insisting on these outside relationships. This was to be it. The very last time."

"It turned out to be just that, didn't it?" Carella said.

"I was *here* at five-thirty," Harrod said. "Check it."

"With whom?"

Harrod hesitated.

"Who were you with, Mr. Harrod?"

"A friend of mine."

"Who?"

"His name is Oliver Walsh. Are you going to hassle him, too?"

"Yes," Carella said, "I'm going to hassle him, too."

Oliver Walsh lived within walking distance of Harrod's apartment. Carella got there at five minutes to midnight. He had not called first to announce himself, and he had warned Harrod not to pick up the phone the moment he left the apartment. Walsh seemed genuinely surprised to find a city detective on his doorstep. He was nineteen or twenty years old, Carella guessed, with a shock of red hair and a spate of freckles across the bridge of his nose. Carella saw all this though the wedge in the partially opened door; Walsh would not take off the night chain till Carella showed his shield and his plastic-encased I.D. card.

"I thought you might be a burglar or something," Walsh said.

"Mr. Walsh," Carella said, "I'll tell you why I'm here. I want to know where you were between five-thirty and six o'clock tonight."

"Why?" Walsh said at once.

"Were you here at home?" Carella asked, dodging the question.

"No."

"Then where were you?"

"Why are you asking me?"

"Mr. Walsh," Carella said, "someone's been murdered. All I want to know . . ."

"Well, Jesus . . . you don't think . . ."

107

"Where were you?"

"Between . . . between . . . what time did you say?"

"Five-thirty and six."

". . . th a friend of mine," Walsh said, and looked enormously relieved.

"What's your friend's name?"

"Alex Harrod. His phone number is Quinn 7–6430; call him. Go ahead, call him. He'll tell you where I was."

"Where was that?"

"What?"

Where were you with your friend Alex Harrod?"

"At his apartment. Five-eleven Jacaranda, third floor rear. Apartment Thirty-two. Go ahead, call him."

"What time did you get there?"

"About twenty after five. He was just coming home from work."

"How long did you stay there?"

"I left about nine-thirty."

"Did you leave the apartment at any time?"

"No, I did not."

"Did Harrod?"

"No, we were there together."

"How long have you know Harrod?"

"We met only recently."

"When?"

"On Christmas Eve."

"Where?"

"At a party."

"Where was the party?"

"Here in the Quarter."

"Where in the Quarter?"

"In Llewlyn Mews. A man named Daniel Corbett was giving a party, and a friend of mine asked me to go with him."

"Had you known Corbett before then?"

"No, I met him that night."

"And that's when you met Harrod, too, is that right?"

"That's right."

"Have you spoken to him since you left his apartment tonight?"

"No, I haven't."

"We can check with the phone company for any calls made from his number to yours."

"Check," Walsh said. "I left him at nine-thirty, and I

haven't spoken to him since. Who got murdered? It wasn't Alex, was it?"

"No, it wasn't Alex," Carella said. "Thank you for your time, Mr. Walsh."

8

The way they reconstructed it later, the killer had gone after the wrong person. The mistake was reasonable; even Carella had made the same mistake earlier. The killer must have been watching her for the past several days, and when he saw her—or the person he *assumed* was Hillary Scott—coming out of the Stewart City apartment building at eight-thirty Wednesday morning, he followed her all the way to the subway kiosk and then attempted to stab her with what Denise Scott later described as "the biggest damn knife I've ever seen in my life."

Minutes after Denise rushed into the apartment with the front of her black cloth coat and her white satin blouse slashed, Hillary called first the local precinct and then Carella at home. He and Hawes got there an hour later. The patrolmen from Midtown South were already there, wondering what they were supposed to do. They asked Carella whether they should report this to their precinct as a 10–24—an "Assault Past"—or would the Eight-Seven take care of it? Carella explained that the attack might have been linked to a homicide they were working, and the patrolmen should forget about it. The patrolmen seemed unconvinced.

"What about the paper?" one of them asked. "Who'll take care of the paper?"

"I will," Carella said.

"So then maybe *we* get in a jam," the second patrolman said.

"If you want to file, go ahead and file," Carella said.

"As what? A Ten-twenty-four?"

"That's what it was."

"Where do we say it *was?*"

"What do you mean?"

"The guy tried to stab her outside the subway on Masters. But she didn't call us till she got back here. So what do we put down as the scene?"

"Here," Carella said. "This is where you responded, isn't it?"

"Yeah, but this ain't where it happened."

"So let *me* file, okay?" Carella said. "Don't worry about it."

"You ain't got a sergeant like we got," the first patrolman said.

"Look, I want to talk to the victim," Carella said. "I told you this is a homicide we're working, so how about letting *me* file, and then you won't have to worry about it."

"Get his name and shield number," the second patrolman advised.

"Detective/Second Grade Stephen Louis Carella," Carella said patiently, "Eighty-seventh Squad. My shield number is seven-one-four, five-six-three-two."

"You got that?" the second patrolman asked his partner.

"I got it," the first patrolman said, and they both left the apartment, still concerned about what their sergeant might say.

Denise Scott was in a state of numbed shock. Her face was pale; her lips were trembling; she had not taken off her coat—as if somehow it still afforded her protection against the assailant's knife. Hillary brought her a whopping snifter of brandy, and when she had taken several swallows of it and the color had returned to her cheeks, she seemed ready to talk about what had happened. What had happened was really quite simple. Someone had grabbed her from behind as she was starting down the steps to the subway station, pulled her over backward, and then slashed at the front of her coat with the biggest damn knife she'd ever seen in her life. She'd hit out at him with her bag, and she'd begun screaming, and the man had turned and begun running when someone started up the steps from below.

"It was a man, you're sure of that?" Carella said.

"Positive."

"What did he look like?" Hawes asked.

"Black hair and brown eyes. A very narrow face," Denise said.

"How old?"

"Late twenties, I'd say."

"Would you recognize him if you saw him again?"

"In a minute."

"Did he say anything to you?"

"Not a word. He just pulled me around and tried to stab me. Look what he did to my coat and blouse," she said, and eased the torn blouse aside to study the sloping top of her left breast. Hawes seemed very interested in whether or not the knife had penetrated her flesh. He stared at the V opening of her blouse with all the scrutiny of an assistant medical examiner. "I was just lucky, that's all," Denise said, and let the blouse fall back into place.

"He was after *me*," Hillary said.

Carella did not ask her why she thought so; he was thinking exactly the same thing.

"Let me have the coat," she said.

"What?" her sister said.

"Your coat. Let me have it."

Denise took off the coat. The knife thrust had torn the blouse over her left breast. Beneath the gaping satiny slash, Hawes could glimpse a promise of Denise's flesh, a milkier white against the off white of the satin. Hillary held the black coat against her own breasts like a phantom lover. Closing her eyes, she began to sway the way she had after she'd kissed Carella. Hawes looked at her and then looked at her sister and decided he would rather go to bed with Denise than with Hillary. Then he decided the exact opposite. Then he decided both of them wouldn't be bad together, at the same time, in the king-sized bed in his apartment. Carella, not being psychic, didn't know that everybody in the world had threesomes in mind this holiday season. Hillary, claiming to be what Carella knew he wasn't, began intoning in a voice reminiscent of the one she'd used after she'd kissed him, "Tape, you stole, tape," the same old routine.

Befuddled, Hawes watched her; he had never caught her act before. Denise, used to the ways of mediums, yawned. The brandy was reaching her. She seemed to have forgotten that less than an hour ago someone had tried to dispatch her to that great beyond her sister was now presumably tapping— Hillary had said it was a ghost who'd killed Gregory Craig, and now the same ghost had tried to kill her sister, and her black overcoat was giving off emanations that seemed to indicate either something or nothing at all.

"Hemp," she said.

Carella wasn't sure whether or not she was clearing her throat.

"Hemp," she said again. "Stay."

He hadn't planned on leaving, so he didn't know what the hell she meant.

"Hemp, stay," she said. "Hempstead. Hampstead."

Carella distinctively felt the hair on the back of his neck bristling. Hawes, watching Denise—who now crossed her legs recklessly and grinned at him in brandy-inspired abandon— felt only a bristling somewhere in the area of his groin.

"Mass," Hillary intoned, her eyes still closed, her body swaying, the black overcoat clutched in her hands. "Mass. Massa*chu*setts. Hampstead, Massachusetts," and Carella's mouth dropped open.

Hillary opened her eyes and stared blankly at him. His own stare was equally blank. Like a pair of blind idiot savants sharing the same mysterious knowledge, they stared at each other across an abyss no wider than three feet, but writhing with whispering demons and restless corpses. His feet were suddenly cold. He stared at her unblinkingly, and she stared back, and he could swear her eyes were on fire, the deep brown lighted from within with all the reds and yellows of glittering opals.

"Someone drowned in Hampstead, Massachusetts," she said.

She said this directly to him, ignoring Hawes and her sister. And Carella, knowing full well that she had lived with Craig for the past year and more, knowing, too, that he might have told her all about the drowning of his former wife two miles from where he was renting the haunted house he made famous in *Deadly Shades,* nonetheless believed that the knowledge had come to her from the black overcoat she held in her hands.

When she said, "We'll go to Massachusetts, you and I," he knew that they would because Craig's wife had drowned up there three summers ago, and now three more people were dead, and another murder attempt had been made—and maybe there *were* ghosts involved after all.

They had hoped to get there by one in the afternoon, a not unrealistic estimate in that they left the city at a little after ten and Hampstead—by the map—was no more than 200 miles to the northeast. The roads outside the city were bone-dry; the storm that had blanketed Isola had left the surrounding areas untouched. It was only when they entered Massachusetts that they encountered difficulty. Whereas earlier Carella had maintained a steady fifty-five miles an hour in keeping with the federal energy-saving speed limit, he now eased off on the accelerator and hoped he would average thirty. Snow was not the problem; any state hoping for skiers during the winter months made certain the roads were plowed and scraped the instant the first snowflake fell. But the temperature had dropped to eighteen degrees Fahrenheit, and the roadside snow that had been melting during the midmorning hours had now frozen into a thin slick that covered the asphalt from median divider to shoulder and made driving treacherous and exhausting.

They reached Hampstead at two-twenty-five that afternoon. The sky was overcast, and a harsh wind blew in over the ocean, rattling the wooden shutters on the seaside buildings. The town seemed to have crawled up out of the Atlantic like some prehistoric thing seeking the sun, finding instead a rocky, inhospitable coastline and collapsing upon it in disappointment and exhaustion. The ramshackle buildings on the waterfront were uniformly gray, their weather-beaten shingles evoking a time when Hampstead was a small fishing village and men went down to the sea in ships. There were still nets and lobster pots in evidence, but the inevitable crush of progress had threaded through the town a gaudy string of motels and fast-food joints that thoroughly blighted what could not have been a particularly cheerful place to begin with.

The Common, such as it was, consisted of a sere rectangle of untended lawn surrounded by the town's municipal buildings and a four-story brick hotel that called itself the Hampstead Arms. The tawdry tinsel of the season encompassed the square like a squadron of dancing girls in sequins and spangles. An unlighted Christmas tree was in the center of the Common, looking rather like a sodden sea gull that had lost its bearings. Carella parked the car, and together he and Hillary walked to the Town Hall, where he hoped to find the Coroner's Office and the records pertaining to the death of Gregory Craig's former wife. Hillary was wearing a bulky raccoon coat, a brown woolen hat pulled down over her ears, brown gloves, brown boots, and the same outfit she'd been wearing in her sister's apartment that morning: a tweedy beige skirt flecked with threads of green and brown, a turtleneck the color of bitter chocolate, and a green cardigan sweater with leather buttons. Carella was wearing much of the finery that had been given to him two days earlier: a pair of dark gray flannel slacks from Fanny, a red plaid flannel shirt from April, a tweed sports jacket the color of smoked herring from Teddy, a dark blue car coat with a fleece lining and a fake fur collar, also from Teddy, and a pair of fur-lined gloves from Mark. His feet were cold; he had put on loafers this morning, not expecting to be trodding the streets of an oceanfront town in Massachusetts, where the temperature lurked somewhere just above zero and the wind came in off the Atlantic like the revenge of every seaman ever lost in those dark waters offshore. As they crossed the Common,

Hillary nodded and said, "Yes, I knew it would look like this."

Hampstead's Town Hall was a white clapboard building with a gray shingled roof. It faced westward, away from the ocean, shielding the sidewalk outside from the fierce Atlantic blasts. All the lights were on in defense against the afternoon gloom; they beckoned like beacons to lost mariners. Inside, the building was as toasty warm as a general store with a potbellied stove. Carella studied the information board in the lobby, a black rectangle with white plastic letters and numbers on it, announcing the various departments and the rooms in which they might be found. There was no listing for a Coroner's Office. He settled for the Town Clerk's Office and spoke there to a woman who sounded a lot like the late President Kennedy. She told him that the Coroner's Office was located in Hampstead General Hospital, which was about two miles to the northeast, just the other side of the Bight. Reluctant to face the frozen waste yet another time, Carella nonetheless walked with Hillary to where he'd parked the car and then drove due north along an oceanfront road that curved past what appeared to be a large saltwater pond, but which was identified by a roadside sign as HAMPSTEAD BIGHT.

"That's where she drowned," Hillary said. "Stop the car."

"No," Carella said. "First let's find out *how* she drowned."

The coroner was a man in his late sixties, as pale and as thin as a cadaver, with a fringe of graying hair around his flaking bald pate. He was wearing a threadbare brown sweater, rumpled brown slacks, a white shirt with a frayed collar, and a tie the color of cow dung. His desk was cluttered with a sheaf of loosely scattered file folders and a black plastic sign that announced his name in white letters: MR. HIRAM HOLLISTER. Carella spoke to him alone; it was one thing to bring your medium with you when you went calling on ghosts; it was quite another to conduct official business in the presence of a startlingly beautiful twenty-two-year-old wearing a raccoon coat that made her look cozily cuddlesome. Hillary waited on a bench in the corridor outside.

"I'm investigating three possibly linked homicides in Isola," Carella said, showing his shield. "One of the victims was a man named Gregory Craig, who . . ."

"What's that say there?" Hollister asked, peering at the gold shield with its blue enameling and its embossed city seal.

"Detective," Carella said.

"Oh, detective, yup," Hollister said.

"One of the victims was a man named Gregory Craig. His

115

former wife, Stephanie Craig, drowned in Hampstead Bight three summers ago. Your office concluded that the death was accidental. I wonder if I might . . ."

"Three summers ago, yup," Hollister said.

"Do you remember the case?"

"No, but I remember three summers ago, all right. That was the year we got all that rain."

"Would you have a record of what happened? I'm assuming there was an inquest . . ."

"Oh, yes, there woulda been in a drowning."

"Stephanie Craig," Carella said. "Does that name mean anything to you?"

"Not offhand. We get tourists here, you know, they don't know how tricky the currents can be. We get our share of drownings, I'll tell you, same as any other coastal community."

"How about Gregory Craig?"

"Don't recollect him either."

"He wrote a book called *Deadly Shades*."

"Haven't read it."

"About a house in this town."

"Nope, don't know it."

Carella thought briefly about the illusiveness of fame. Behind his desk Hollister was nodding as though he had suddenly remembered something he had not earlier revealed.

"Yup," he said.

Carella waited.

"Lots of rain that summer. Washed away the dock outside Logan's Pier."

"Mr. Hollister," Carella said, "where would I find a record of the inquest?"

"Right down the hall," Hollister said, and looked at his watch. "But it's getting on three o'clock, and I want to start home before the storm hits. Supposed to be getting at least six inches, did you know that?"

"No, I didn't," Carella said, and looked at his own watch. "If you'll pull the folder for me," he said, "I can take a look at it and then leave it on your desk, if that would be all right with you."

"Well," Hollister said.

"I can sign a receipt for it in my official capacity as . . ."

"Nope, don't need a receipt," Hollister said. "Just don't want it getting all messed up and out of place."

"I'll be very careful with it," Carella said.

116

"Get out-of-state police in here every so often," Hollister said, "they don't know about neatness and orderliness."

"I can understand that, sir," Carella said, figuring a "sir" wouldn't hurt at this uneasy juncture. "But I'm used to handling files, and I promise I'll return the folder in exactly the condition I receive it. Sir," he added.

"Suppose it'd be all right," Hollister said, and eased himself out of his swivel chair, surprising Carella with a six-foot-four frame that should have belonged to a basketball player. He followed Hollister down the corridor, past Hillary, who sat on the bench and looked up at him inquiringly, and then into an office succinctly marked RECORDS on the frosted glass panel of its door. The office was lined with dusty wooden file cabinets that would have fetched handsome prices in any of Isola's antique shops.

"How do you spell that last name?" Hollister asked.

"C-R-A-I-G" Carella said, and thought again about fame, and wondered if somewhere in America there was at this very moment someone asking how you spelled Hemingway or Faulkner or even Harold Robbins.

"C-R-A-I-G," Hollister said, and then went to one of the file cabinets, and opened the drawer, and kept spelling the name over and over to himself as he leafed through the folders.

"Stephanie?" he asked.

"Stephanie," Carella said.

"Here it is," Hollister said, and yanked out an inch-thick folder, and studied the name on it again before handing it to Carella. "Just put it here on top the cabinet when you're through with it. I don't want you trying to file it again, hear?"

"Yes, sir," Carella said.

"Mess up the files that way," Hollister said.

"Yes, sir."

"You can use the desk over there near the windows if you like, take off your coat, make yourself comfortable. Who's that lady outside looks like a grizzly bear?"

"She's helping me with the case," Carella said.

"You can bring her in, too, if that suits you; no sense her freezing her butt off in the hallway. Terrible draft in that hallway."

"Yes, sir, thank you," Carella said.

"Well, that's it, I guess," Hollister said, and shrugged and left Carella alone in the room. Carella poked his head outside

117

the door. Hillary was still cooling her heels on the bench, impatiently jiggling one of her crossed legs.

"Come on in," he said, and she rose instantly and came down the corridor, the heels of her boots clicking on the wooden floor.

"What've you got?" she asked.

"Record of the inquest."

"We'd learn more at the Bight," she said.

Carella turned on the desk's gooseneck lamp and then pulled up a chair for Hillary. She did not take off the raccoon coat. Outside, it was already beginning to snow. The clock on the wall ticked off the time: seven minutes to three.

"I want to make this fast," Carella said, "and get out of here before the storm hits."

"We have to go to the Bight," Hillary said. "I'm here because I want to see the Bight. And the house Greg rented."

"If there's time," he said.

"We won't get out in any event," she said. "They've already closed Route Forty-four."

"How do you know that?" he asked, and she gave him a weary look. "Well . . . let's hurry, anyway," he said. "Did you want to look at this with me? Is there anything here that . . ."

"I want to touch the papers," she said.

After her performance with her sister's coat, he knew better than to scoff at her request. In the car on the drive to Massachusetts, she had tried to explain to him the powers she and others like her possessed. He had listened intently as she told him about extrasensory perception and psychometry in particular. She defined this as the ability to measure with the sixth sense the flux—or electromagnetic radiation—from another person, most often by touching an object owned or worn by that person. People blessed—"Or sometimes cursed," she said—with this gift were capable of garnering information about the past and the present and sometimes, in the case of particularly talented psychometrists, even the future. She explained that one might consider time, from the psychic point of view, as a huge phonograph record with millions upon millions of ridges and grooves, containing millennia of recorded data. The psychic, in a sense, was someone with the extraordinary power of being able to lift the metaphoric cartridge of a record player and drop the needle into any of the grooves, thereby reproducing in the mind any of the preserved information on the disc. She was not quite certain how this worked concerning future events; she had never been able to prophesy with any amount of accuracy something that was *about* to happen. Clairvoyance, clairaudience, and clairsentience all were talents beyond her meager capabilities. But she was entirely certain of her power to intuit correctly, from any object's electromagnetic leak of energy, the events—past or present—identified with that object. She had been able to do this with her sister's coat yesterday because the coat had come into contact with the killer's knife, and the knife had been held in the killer's hand, and the flux had been strong enough to transfer itself from human being to object to yet another object. Her dissertation, soberly delivered, did much to convince Carella even further that she *did* possess powers he was incapable of reasoning away.

Sitting at the desk beside her now, he opened the case folder and began reading. She did not read along with him. She simply touched the right-hand corner of each page, the way one might have if attempting to dog-ear it, holding the page between her thumb and index finger, feeling it as she might have felt a fabric sample, her eyes closed, her body slightly swaying on the chair beside him. She was wearing a heady perfume he had not noticed on the car ride up. He assumed her psychometric concentration was creating emanations of her own by way of body heat that hyped the scent of the perfume.

According to the Coroner's Inquest held on the sixteenth day of September, three weeks after the fatal drowning three summers ago, Stephanie Craig had been swimming alone in Hampstead Bight between three and three-fifty in the afternoon, when, according to observers on the shore, she suddenly disappeared below the surface. She came up twice, struggling and gasping for breath each time, but when she went under for the third time, she did not surface again. One of the eyewitnesses suggested at the inquest that Mrs. Craig (apparently she still used the "Mrs." form of address four years after her divorce from Craig) may have been seized from below by a shark "or some other kind of fish," but the Board rejected this at once, citing the fact that there had been no blood in the water and perhaps mindful of the many recent books and motion pictures that had done little to encourage the flow of tourists to oceanside communities; the last thing on earth Hampstead needed was a shark scare—or any *other* kind of fish scare.

The Board had conducted its inquiry meticulously, eliciting

119

from Mrs. Craig's handyman the information that she'd left for the beach at two-thirty that afternoon, taking with her a towel and a shoulder-slung handbag and telling him she planned to "walk on over to the Bight for a little swim." She was wearing, as he clearly recalled, a blue bikini bathing suit and sandals. Witnesses at the beach recalled seeing her walking to the water's edge, testing the water with her toes, and then coming back from the shoreline to put down her sandals, her towel, and her handbag. One of the witnesses mentioned that it was the "first darn sunny day we'd had in weeks," a comment that must have done little to gladden the hearts of the two Chamber of Commerce members on the Board.

Stephanie Craig went into the water for her swim at 3:00 P.M. The Bight was even calmer that day than it normally was. Protected by a natural-rock breakwater that crashed with ocean waves on its eastern side, fringed with a white sand beach rare in these parts, it was a safe current-free place for swimming and a favorite among locals and tourists alike. There were sixty-four people on the beach that day. Only a dozen of them witnessed the drowning. Each and every one of them told exactly the same story. She suddenly went under, and she drowned. Period. The Medical Examiner's report stated that there were no contusions, lacerations, or bruises anywhere on the body, dismissing once and for all the notion that a shark "or some other kind of fish" had seized her from below. The report further stated that the body had been delivered to the morgue clad only in the panties of the bikini bathing suit, the bra top apparently having been lost in Mrs. Craig's struggle to save herself from drowning. Findings for drugs or alcohol had been negative. The physician conducting the examination could not state whether a cramp had been the cause of her sudden inability to stay afloat, but the board nonetheless decided that the probable cause of the accident was "a severe cramp or series of cramps that rendered Mrs. Craig powerless in water estimated on that day to have been twenty feet deep where she was swimming." An eyewitness on the beach said that she went under for the last time at ten minutes to four; that meant she'd been swimming for close to an hour in waters not known for their cordial temperatures. But Stephanie Craig had been the winner of three gold medals on Holman University's swimming team, and the Board's report made no mention of this fact.

Carella closed the folder. Hillary passed her hands over the binder and then opened her eyes and said, "It wasn't an accident. Whoever typed this report *knows* it wasn't an accident."

Carella checked the report's first and last pages to see if there was a typist's name or initials anywhere on them. There was not. He made a mental note to call Hollister and find out who had done the typing.

"I want to go to the Bight now," Hillary said. "May we go, please? Before it gets too dark?"

It was almost too dark when they got there. Whatever light still lingered on the horizon was diffused by the falling snow, which made visibility and footing equally uncertain. They stood on the beach and looked out over the water. Stephanie Craig had drowned some fifty feet from shore, just ten yards within the breakwater protection afforded by the curving natural rock ledge. At Hillary's insistence, they walked out onto the breakwater now. It was shaped like a fishhook, the shank jutting out from the shore at a northeasterly angle, the rocks at the farthest end curving back upon themselves to form a natural cove. On the ocean side, waves crashed in against the ledge as if determined to pound it to rubble. But the cove on the bay side was as protected as the larger crescent of beach had been, and here only spume and spray intimidated the flying snowflakes. A rusting iron ladder was fastened to the ledge above the cove. Hillary turned her back to it, and Carella realized all at once that she was planning to go down to the stony beach below. He grabbed her arm and said, "Hey, no."

"It's safe down there," she said. "The ocean's on the other side."

He looked below. The cove did seem safe enough. On the ocean side, towering waves furiously pounded the ledge, but in the protected little cove below he would have trusted his ten-year-old daughter with a rubber duck. He preceded Hillary down the ladder and then turned away circumspectly when she climbed down after him, her skirt whipping about her legs and thighs. There was no wind below. A small cave yawned behind the stony beach, eroded into the ledge. Inside it, they could dimly perceive a beached dinghy painted a green that was flaking and stained red and yellow below its rusting oarlocks. Hillary stopped stock-still just outside the opening to the cave.

"What is it?" Carella said.

"He was out here," she said.

121

"Who?"

The light was fading rapidly; he should have taken his flashlight from the glove compartment of the car, but he hadn't. The cave seemed not in the least bit inviting. He had always considered spelunkers the choicest sorts of maniacs, and he feared ever being trapped in a small space, unable to move either forward or backward. But he followed Hillary into the cave, ducking his head to avoid banging it on the low ceiling, squinting into the darkness beyond the dinghy. The cave was shallow; it ended abruptly several feet beyond the boat. Its sloping walls were wet. Hillary touched one of the rusting oarlocks and then pulled her hand back as if she'd received an electric shock.

"No," she said.

"What is it?"

"No," she said, backing away from the boat. "Oh, no, God, please, no."

"What the hell is it?"

She did not answer. She shook her head and backed out of the cave. She was climbing the ladder when he came out onto the stone-strewn beach behind her. When she reached the ledge above, the wind caught at her skirt, whipping it about her long legs. He climbed up after her. She was running along the breakwater now, the waves crashing in on her left, heading for the crescent beach beyond which he'd parked the car. He ran after her, out of breath, almost losing his footing on the rocks, almost realizing his second wildest fear, that of drowning. When he got to the car, she was already inside it, her arms folded over the front of the raccoon coat, her body trembling.

"What happened back there?" he said.

"Nothing."

"When you touched that boat . . ."

"Nothing," she said.

He started the car. There were at least two inches of snow in the parking lot. The dashboard clock read 4:00 P.M. He turned on the radio at once, hoping to catch the local news, and listened first to a report on the president's new plan for fighting inflation, then to a report on the latest trouble in the Middle East, and finally to a report on the weather. The storm that had inundated the city had finally reached Massachusetts and was expected to dump somewhere between eight and ten inches of snow before morning. Route 44 was closed, and the turnpike south and west was treacherous. Traveler's advisories were in effect; the state's Highway Department had asked that all vehicles be kept off the roads to allow the plows free access.

"We'd better get back to town," he said, "see if we can't get a couple of rooms for the night."

"No," she said. She was still shivering. "I want to see the house Greg rented that summer."

"I don't want to get stuck out here in the middle of no—"

"It's on the way," she said. "Two miles from the Bight. Isn't that what she told you? Isn't that what his daughter told you?"

Abigail Criag had said, *She drowned in the Bight, two miles from where my father was renting his famous haunted house.* Partial believer that he was, Carella was willing to accept the fact that Hillary could not have known of his conversation with Craig's daughter and had therefore divined it through her psychic powers. But skeptic that he *still* was, he realized Hillary was no doubt familiar with the book Craig had written about the house, so wasn't it now reasonable to assume he'd described it in detail, right down to its geographical location?

"Two miles from the Bight could be two miles in either direction," he said. "I don't want to be driving out into the Atlantic Ocean."

"No, it's on the way to town," she said.

"Did he say so in his book?"

"I recognized it when we passed it," she said.

"You didn't answer my question."

"No, he did not give its exact location in the book."

"Why didn't you say something when we passed it?"

"Because the field was so strong."

"What field?"

"The electromagnetic field."

"So strong that it silenced you?"

"So strong that it *frightened* me."

"But the Bight didn't, huh? When we passed the bight . . ."

"The Bight was only where she drowned. The house . . ."

She shivered again and hunkered down inside her coat. He had never really heard a person's teeth chattering; he'd always thought that was for fiction. But her teeth were truly chattering now; he could hear the tiny click of them above the hum of the car heater.

"What *about* the house?" he said.

123

"I have to see it. The house was the beginning. The house was where it all started."

"Where all *what* started?"

"The four murders."

"Four?" he said. "There've only been three."

"Four," she repeated.

"Gregory Craig, Marian Esposito, Daniel Corbett . . ."

"And Stephanie Craig," she said.

9

The house was on the edge of the ocean, 1.8 miles from the Bight, according to the odometer. He parked the car in a rutted sand driveway covered with snow and flanked by withered beach grass and plum. A solitary pine, its branches weighted by the snow upon them, stood to the left of the entrance door like a giant Napoleonic soldier outside Moscow. The house was almost entirely gray: weathered gray shingles on all of its sides; gray shingles of a darker hue on its roof; the door, the shutters, and the window trim all painted a gray that was flaking and faded. A brick chimney climbed the two stories on its northern end, contributing a column of color as red as blood, a piercing vertical shriek against the gray of the house and the white of the whirling snow. This time he had remembered to take along the flashlight. He played it first on a small sign in the window closest to the entrance door. The sign advised that the house was for rent or for sale and provided the name and address of the real estate agent to be contacted. He moved the light to the tarnished doorknob and then tried the knob. The door was locked.

"That's that," he said.

Hillary put her hand on the knob. She closed her eyes. He waited, never knowing *what* the hell to expect when she touched something. A snowflake landed on the back of his neck and melted down his collar.

"There's a back door," she said.

They trudged through the snow around the side of the house, past a thorny patch of brambles, and then onto a gray wooden porch on the ocean side. The wind here had banked the snow against the storm door. He kicked the snow away with the side of his shoe, yanked open the storm door, and then tried the knob on the inner door.

"Locked," he said. "Let's get back to town."

Hillary reached for the knob. Carella sighed. She held the knob for what seemed an inordinately long time, the wind whistling in over the ocean and lashing the small porch, the storm door banging against the side of the house. When she released the knob, she said, "There's a key behind the drainpipe."

Carella played the light over the drainpipe. The spout was perhaps eight inches above the ground. He felt behind it with his hand. Fastened to the back of the spout was one of those magnetic little key holders designed to make entrance by burglars even easier than it had to be. He slid open the lid on the metal container, took out a key, and tried it on the lock. It slid easily into the keyway; when he twisted it, he heard the tumblers fall with a small oiled click. He tried the knob again, and the door opened. Fumbling on the wall to the right of the door, he found a light switch and flicked it on. He took a step into the room; Hillary, behind him, closed the door.

They were standing in a living room furnished in what might have been termed Beach House Haphazard. A sofa covered with floral-patterned slipcovers was on the window wall overlooking the ocean. Two mismatched upholstered easy chairs faced the sofa like ugly suitors petitioning for the hand of a princess. A stained oval braided rug was on the floor between the sofa and the chairs, and a cobbler's bench coffee table rested on it slightly off center. An upright piano was on a wall bearing two doors, one leading to the kitchen, the other to a pantry. A flight of steps at the far end of the room led to the upper story of the house.

"This isn't it," Hillary said.

"What do you mean?"

"This isn't the house Greg wrote about."

"I thought you said . . ."

"I said it *started* here. But this isn't the house in *Deadly Shades.*"

"How do you know?"

"There are no ghosts in this house," she said flatly. "There never *were* any ghosts in this house."

They went through it top to bottom nonetheless. Hillary's manner was calm, almost detached. She went through the place like a disinterested buyer whose husband was trying to force upon her an unwanted purchase—until they reached the basement. In the basement, and Carella was becoming used to these sudden shifts of psychic mood, she bristled at the sight of a closed door. Her hands began flailing the air, the fingers on each widespread like those of a blind person searching for obstacles. Trembling, she approached the door. She lifted the primitive latch and entered a shelf-lined room that contained the house's furnace. Carella was aware all at once that the house was frighteningly cold. His feet were leaden; his hands

126

were numb. On one of the shelves were a diver's mask, a pair of rubber fins, and an oxygen tank. Hillary approached the shelf, but she did not touch anything on it. Again, as she had with the dinghy in the cave, she backed away and said, "No, oh, God, no."

He felt something almost palpable in that room, but he knew better than to believe he was intuiting whatever Hillary was. His response was hard-nosed, that of a detective in one of the world's largest cities, compounded of years of experience and miles of empirical deduction, seasoned with a pinch of guesswork and a heaping tablespoon of hope—but hope was the thing with feathers. Stephanie Craig, an expert swimmer, had drowned in the Bight in a calmer sea than anyone could remember that summer. At least one of the witnesses had suggested that she'd been seized from below by a shark or some other kind of fish. In the basement room of the house her former husband, Gregory, had rented for the summer, they had just stumbled upon a diver's gear. Wasn't it possible . . . ?

"It was Greg," Hillary said. "Greg drowned her."

At the Hampstead Arms they booked a pair of connecting rooms for the night. As Carella dialed his home in Riverhead, he could hear Hillary on the phone next door. He did not know whom she was calling. He knew only that in the car on the way back to town she had refused to amplify her blunt accusation. Fanny answered the phone on the fourth ring.

"Hi," he said, "I'm stuck up here."

"And where's up there?" Fanny asked.

"I asked Cotton to call . . ."

"He didn't."

"I'm in Massachusetts."

"Ah," Fanny said. "And what, may I ask, are you doing in Massachusetts?"

"Checking out haunted houses."

"Your Italian sense of humor leaves much to be desired," Fanny said. "Teddy'll have a fit. She's been thinking you were killed in some dark alley."

"Tell her I'm all right and I'll call again in the morning."

"It won't mollify her."

"Then tell her I love her."

"If you love her, then what the hell are you doing in Massachusetts?"

"Is everything all right there?"

"Everything's fine and dandy."

127

"It hasn't snowed again, has it?"

"Not a flake."

"It's already snowed eight inches up here."

"Serves you right," Fanny said, and hung up.

He dialed Hawes at the squadroom and got him on the third ring.

"You were supposed to call and tell my wife I went to Massachusetts," he said.

"Shit," Hawes said.

"You forgot."

"It was jumping today. Three guys tried to stick up a bank on Culver and Tenth. Locked themselves inside when the alarm went off, tried to hold off the whole damn Police Department. We finally flushed them out about four o'clock."

"Anybody hurt?"

"One of the tellers had a heart attack. But that was it. I'm glad you called. We got something on the jewelry. A pawnbroker called the squadroom while I was out playing cops and robbers. Runs a shop on Ainsley and Third."

"Yeah, go ahead."

"I called him back the minute I got in. Turns out some guy was in there this afternoon trying to hock the diamond pendant. Just a second, here's the list." The line went silent. Carella visualized Hawes running his finger down the list Hillary Scott had provided. "Yeah," Hawes said, "here it is. 'One pear-shaped diamond pendant set in platinum with an eighteen-inch chain of eighteen-karat gold.' "

"What was it valued at?"

"Thirty-five hundred."

"Who pawned it?"

"*Tried* to pawn it. The broker offered sixteen hundred, and the guy accepted and then balked when he was asked for identification. They have to get identification, you know, for when they send their list of transactions to us."

"And the guy refused to show it?"

"All the broker wanted was a driver's license. The guy said he didn't have a driver's license."

"So what happened?"

"He picked up the pendant and left."

"Great," Carella said.

"It's not all that bad. The minute he left the shop, the broker checked the flyer we sent around and spotted the pendant on it. That's when he called here. There was a number on the flyer, you remember . . ."

"Yeah, so what happened?"

"He told me the guy had his hands all over the glass top of the jewelry counter. He figured we could maybe lift some prints from it. He's a pretty smart old guy."

"Did you go down there?"

"Just got back, in fact. Left a team there to dust the jewelry counter and the doorknob and anything else the guy may have touched. Dozens of people go in and out of that place every day, Steve, but maybe we'll get lucky."

"Yeah, maybe. What'd the guy look like?"

"He fits the description. Young guy with black hair and brown eyes."

"When will the lab boys let you know?"

"They're on it now."

"What does that mean? Tomorrow morning?"

"I told them it's a homicide. Maybe we'll get some quick action."

"Okay, let me know if you get anything. I'm at the Hampstead Arms; you want to write down this number?"

"Let me get a pencil," Hawes said. "Never a fuckin pencil around when you need one."

He gave Hawes the number of the hotel and the room extension and then filled him in on what he'd learned at the Coroner's Office. He did not mention any of Hillary's psychic deductions. When he hung up, it was close to six o'clock. He looked up Hiram Hollister's home number in the local directory and dialed it.

"Hello?" a woman said.

"Mr. Hollister, please."

"Who's calling?"

"Detective Carella."

"Just a moment."

He waited. When Hollister came onto the phone, he said, "Hello, Mr. Carella. Get what you were looking for?"

"Yes, thank you," Carella said. "Mr. Hollister, I wonder if you can tell me who typed that report filed by the inquest board."

"Typed it?"

"Yes."

"Typed it? Do you mean the *typist* who typed it?"

"Yes, sir."

"Would've been the inquest stenographer, I suppose."

"And who was that?"

"This was three summers ago," Hollister said.

129

"Yes."

"Would've been Maude Jenkins," he said. "Yup. Three summers ago would've been Maude."

"Where can I reach her?"

"She's in the phone book. It'll be listed under Harold Jenkins; that's her husband's name."

"Thank you, Mr. Hollister."

He hung up and consulted the telephone directory again. He found a listing for Harold Jenkins and a second listing for Harold Jenkins, Jr. He tried the first number and got an elderly man, who said Carella was probably looking for his daughter-in-law and started to give him the number for Harold Jenkins, Jr. Carella told him he had the number, thanked him, and then dialed the second listing.

"Jenkins," a man's voice said.

"Mr. Jenkins, I'm Detective Carella of the Eighty-seventh Squad in Isola. I wonder if I might speak to your wife, please?"

"My wife? Maude?"

"Yes, sir."

"Well . . . sure," Jenkins said. His voice sounded puzzled. Carella heard him calling to his wife. He waited. In the next room, Hillary Scott was still on the phone.

"Hello?" a woman's voice said.

"Mrs. Jenkins?"

"Yes?"

"This is Detective Carella of the Eighty-seventh Squad in Isola . . ."

"Yes?"

"I'm here in connection with a homicide I'm investigating, and I wonder if you'd mind answering some questions."

"A homicide?"

"Yes. I understand you were the stenographer at the Stephanie Craig inquest three years . . ."

"Yes, I was."

"Did you type up the report?"

"Yes, I took the shorthand transcript, and then I typed it up when the inquest was over. We try to have the same person typing it as took it down. That's because shorthand differs from one person to another, and we don't want mistakes in something as important as an inquest." She hesitated and then said, "But the drowning was accidental."

"So I understand."

"You said homicide. You said you were investigating a homicide."

"Which may or may not be related to the drowning," Carella said. He himself hesitated and then asked, "Mrs. Jenkins, did you yourself have any reason to believe Mrs. Craig's death was anything but accidental?"

"None at all."

"Did you know Mrs. Craig personally?"

"Saw her around town, that's all. She was one of the summer people. Actually, I knew her husband better than I did her. Her *ex*-husband, I should say."

"You knew Gregory Craig?"

"Yes, I did some work for him."

"What kind of work?"

"Typing."

"What did you type for him, Mrs. Jenkins?"

"A book he was working on."

"What book?"

"Oh, you know the book. The one that got to be such a big best-seller later on. The one about ghosts."

"*Deadly Shades?* Was that the title?"

"Not while I was typing it."

"What do you mean?"

"There wasn't any title then."

"There was no title page?"

"Well, there couldn't have been a title page since there weren't any *pages*."

"I'm not following you, Mrs. Jenkins."

"It was all on tape."

"The book was on tape?"

"It wasn't even a *book* actually. It was just Mr. Craig talking about this haunted house. Telling stories about the ghosts in it. All nonsense. It's beyond me how it got to be a best-seller. That house he was renting never had a ghost in it at all. He just made the whole thing up."

"You've been in that house?"

"My sister from Ohio rented it last summer. She'da told me if there'd been any ghosts in it, believe you me."

"This tape Mr. Craig gave you . . ."

"Uh-huh?"

"What happened to it?"

"What do you mean, what happened to it?"

"Did you give it back to him when you finished typing the book?"

"Didn't *finish* typing it. Got about halfway through it, and then the summer ended, and he went back to the city."

"When was this?"

"After Labor Day."

"In September?"

"That's when Labor Day is. Each and every year."

"That would've been after his wife drowned," Carella said.

"Yes, she drowned in August. Late August."

"Was Mr. Craig at the inquest?"

"Didn't need to be. They were divorced, you know. There was no reason to call him for the inquest. Besides, he'd already left Hampstead by then. I forget the actual date of the inquest . . ."

"September sixteenth."

"Yes, well, he was gone by then."

"How much of the book had you finished typing before he left?"

"I told you, it *wasn't* a book. It was just this rambling on about ghosts."

"More or less his *notes* for a book, is that how you'd describe . . . ?"

"No, it was *stories* more than notes. About the candles flickering, you know, and the door being open after someone had locked it. And the woman searching for her husband. Like that. Stories."

"Mr. Craig telling stories about ghosts, is that it?"

"Yes. And using a sort of spooky voice on the tape, do you know? When he was telling the stories. He tried to make it all very dramatic, the business about waking up in the middle of the night and hearing the woman coming down from the attic and then taking a candle and going out into the hall and seeing her there. It was all nonsense, but it was very spooky."

"The stories."

"Yes, and his voice, too."

"By spooky . . ."

"Sort of . . . rasping, I guess. Mr. Craig was a heavy smoker, and his voice was *always* sort of husky. But not like on the tape. I guess he was trying for some kind of effect on the tape. Almost like an actor, you know, telling a spooky story on television. It *sounded* a lot better than it typed up, I can tell you that."

"Mrs. Jenkins, have you read *Deadly Shades?*"

"I guess everybody in this town has read it."

Except Hiram Hollister, Carella thought.

"Was it similar to what you typed from the tape?"

"Well, I didn't type *all* of it."

"The portion you *did* type."

"I didn't have it to compare, but from memory I'd say it was identical to what I typed."

"And you returned the tape to him before he left Hampstead?"

"Yes, I did."

"How long a tape was it?"

"A two-hour cassette."

"How much of it had you typed before he left?"

"Oh, I'd say about half of it."

"An hour's worth, approximately?"

"Yes."

"How many pages did that come to?"

"No more than fifty pages or so."

"Then the full tape would have run to about a hundred pages."

"More or less."

"Mrs. Jenkins, I haven't read the book—would you remember how long it was?"

"In pages?"

"Yes."

"Oh, it was a pretty fat book."

"Fatter than a hundred pages?"

"Oh, yes. Maybe three hundred pages."

"Then there would have been *other* tapes."

"I have no idea. He just gave me the one tape."

"How'd he get in touch with you?"

"I do work for other writers. We get a lot of writers up here in the summer. I guess he asked around and found out about me that way."

"Had you done any work for him before this?"

"No, this was my first job for him."

"And you say there was no title at the time?"

"No title."

"Nothing on the cassette itself?"

"Oh, I see what you mean. Yes, there was. On the label, do you know? Written with a felt-tip pen."

"What was on the label?"

"Ghosts."

"Just the single word 'ghosts'?"

"And his name."

"Craig's name?"

"Yes. 'Ghosts' and then 'Gregory Craig.' "

133

"Then there *was* a title at the time."

"Well, if you want to call it a *title*. But it didn't say, '*By* Gregory Craig'; it was just a way of identifying the cassette, that's all."

"Thank you, Mrs. Jenkins, you've been very helpful," he said.

"Well, all right," she said, and hung up.

He frankly didn't know *how* she'd been helpful, but he guessed maybe she had. During Hillary's trance last Saturday she had mentioned the word "tape" over and again and had linked it with the word "drowning." He had conjured at once the image of a drowning victim whose hands or feet had been bound with tape—a flight of fancy strengthened by the fact that Gregory Craig's hands had been bound behind his back with a wire hanger. In one of Carella's books on legal pathology and toxicology, he had come across a sentence that made him laugh out loud: "If a drowned body is recovered from the water, bound in a manner that could not possibly have been self-accomplished, one might reasonably suspect homicidal intent." Stephanie Craig's body had been unfettered, neither chain, rope, wire *nor* tape trussing her on the day she drowned. But here was another kind of tape entering the picture—and Carella could not forget that Hillary had linked "tape" with "drowning."

She came into his room now without knocking. Her face was flushed; her eyes were glowing.

"I've just been on the phone with a woman named Elise Blair," she said. "She's the real estate agent whose sign was in the window of the house Greg rented."

"What about her?" Carella asked.

"I described the house that was in Greg's book. I described it down to the last nail. She knows the house. It was rented three summers ago to a man from Boston. She wasn't the agent on the deal, but she can check with the realtor who was and get the man's name and address from the lease—if you want it."

"Why would I want it?" Carella asked.

"It was the house in *Shades,* don't you understand?"

"No, I don't."

"It was the house Greg wrote about."

"So?"

"*He* wasn't living in that house; someone *else* was," Hillary said. "I want to go there. I want to see for myself if there are ghosts in that house."

134

10

The real estate agent who had rented the house three summers ago worked out of the back bedroom of her own house on Main Street. They trudged through the snow at a quarter past six, walking past the lighted Christmas tree on the Common, ducking their heads against the snow and the fierce wind. The woman's name was Sally Barton, and she seemed enormously pleased to be playing detective. She had known all along, she told them, that the house Craig wrote about was really the old Loomis house out on the Spit. He had never pinpointed the location, had never even mentioned the town of Hampstead for that matter—something she supposed they should all be grateful for. But she knew it was the Loomis house. "He loved the sea, Frank Loomis did," she said. "The house isn't your typical beach house, but it looks right at home on the Spit. He fell in love with it when he was still living in Salem, had it brought down here stick by stick, put it on the beachfront land he owned."

"Salem?" Carella said. "Here in Massachusetts?"

"Yes," Sally said. "Where they hanged the witches in 1692."

She offered them the key to the house, which she said she'd been unable to rent the summer before, but that had nothing to do with Gregory Craig's ghosts. Not many people outside the town knew that this was the house he'd made famous in his book.

"Don't know how he got away with it," she said. "Claimed it was a true story and then didn't tell anybody where the house actually *was*. Said it was to protect the innocent. What innocent? Frank Loomis has been dead for fifty years, and his two sons are living in California and couldn't care *less* whether there are ghosts in the house. All they're interested in is renting it each summer. Still, I guess he might've been afraid of legal complications. You'd know more about that than I would," she said, and smiled at Carella.

"Well, I'm not a lawyer, ma'am," Carella said, and returned the smile, aware that he'd just been flattered. "I wonder if you can tell me who rented the house three summers ago."

"Yes, I looked for the lease right after you called. It was a man named Jack Rawles."

"What'd he look like?"

"A pleasant-looking person."

"Young, old?"

"In his late twenties, I'd say."

"What color hair?"

"Black."

"Eyes?"

"Brown."

"And his address?"

She gave him the slip of paper on which she had copied Rawles's Commonwealth Avenue address from the lease, and then she said, "It's not an easy house to rent, you know. Frank never did modernize it. There's electricity, of course, but the only heat's from the fireplaces. There're three of them, one in the living room, one in the kitchen, and another in one of the upstairs bedrooms. It's not too bad during the summer, but it's an icebox in the wintertime. Are you sure you want to go out there just now?"

"Yes, we're positive," Hillary said.

"I'd go with you, but I haven't fixed my husband's supper yet."

"We'll return the key to you as soon as we've looked the place over," Carella said.

"There's supposed to be a dead woman there, searching for her husband," Mrs. Barton said.

At a local garage Carella bought a pair of skid chains and asked the attendant to put them on the car while he and Hillary got something to eat at the diner up the street. It was still snowing when they left the town at seven o'clock. The plows were working the streets and the main roads, but he was grateful for the chains when they hit the cutoff that led to the strand of land jutting out into the Atlantic. A sign crusted with snow informed them that this was Albright's Spit, and a sign under it warned that this was a dead-end road. The car struggled through the thick snow, skidding and lurching up what Carella guessed was a packed sand road below. He almost got stuck twice, and when he finally spotted the old house looming on the edge of the sea, he heaved a sigh of relief and parked the car on a relatively level stretch of ground below the sloping driveway. Together, the flashlight lighting their way, he and Hillary made their way to the front door.

"Yes, this is it," Hillary said. "This is the house."

The front door opened into a small entryway facing a flight of stairs that led to the upper story. He found a light switch on the wall to the right of the door and flicked it several times. Nothing happened.

"Wind must've knocked down the power lines," he said, and played the flashlight first on the steps leading upstairs and then around the small entryway. To the right was a door leading to a beamed kitchen. To the left was the living room—what would have been called the "best room" in the days when the house was built. A single thick beam ran the length of the room. There were two windows in the room, one overlooking the ocean, the other on the wall diagonally opposite. The fireplace was not in the exact center of the wall bearing it; the boxed stairwell occupied that space. It was, instead, tucked into the wall beyond, a huge walk-in fireplace with a black iron kettle hanging on a hinge, logs and kindling stacked on the hearth, big black andirons buckled out of shape from the heat of innumerable fires. On the mantel above the fireplace opening, Carella found a pair of candles in pewter candlesticks. He did not smoke; he asked Hillary for a match and lighted both candles.

The room, he now saw, was beautifully furnished in old American antiques, the likes of which could hardly be found for sale anywhere these days, except at exorbitant prices. There were several hurricane lamps around the room, and he lighted these now, and the richly burnished wood of the paneling and the furniture came to flickering life everywhere around him. If there were ghosts in this house, they could not have found a more hospitable place to inhabit. In a brass bucket by the fireplace he found several faded copies of the Hampstead *News*. The dates went back two years, the last time the house had been rented for the summer. He tore the newspapers to shreds, laid a bed of kindling over them, and stacked three hefty logs on top of that. The fire dispelled the lingering chill in the room and, with it, any possible notion that poltergeists might pop out of the woodwork at any moment. Outside, the wind howled in over the ocean and the shutters rattled, but the fire was crackling now, and the lanterns and candles were lighted, and the only ghosts visible were the fire devils dancing on the grate. Carella went out into the kitchen, lighted the candles and lamps there, and

137

then started another fire in the second fireplace. Neither he nor Hillary had yet gone up to the second story of the house.

In one of the kitchen cupboards he found an almost full bottle of scotch. The ice-cube trays in the refrigerator were empty, and the tap water had been turned off. He was starting out of the room with the bottle and two glasses when he noticed the kitchen door was ajar. He put down the glasses and the bottle, went to the door, and opened it all the way. The storm door outside was closed, but the simple slip bolt was unlatched. He threw the bolt and then studied the lock on the inner door. It was a Mickey Mouse lock with a spring latch that any burglar could open in seconds with a strip of celluloid, a knife blade, or a credit card. He locked it nonetheless, yanked on the knob to make certain the door was secure, and then went back into the living room, carrying the bottle of scotch and the two glasses. Hillary was standing at the fireplace. She had taken off the raccoon coat and also the green cardigan sweater. She stood with her legs slightly spread, her booted feet on the stone hearth, her hands extended toward the fire.

"Want some of this?" he said.

"Yes, please."

"Only spirits in the place," he said, intending a joke and surprised when she didn't even smile in response. "We'll have to drink it neat," he said.

He poured generously into both glasses, put the bottle down on the mantel, raised his own glass, said, "Cheers," and took a swallow of whiskey that burned its way clear down to his toes.

"See any ghosts yet?" he asked.

"Not yet."

"Would you know one if you saw one?"

"I'd know one."

"Have you *ever* seen one?"

"No. But I understand the phenomenon."

"How about explaining it to me?"

"You're a skeptic," she said. "I'd be wasting my time."

"Try me."

"No, I'd rather not."

"Okay," he said, and shrugged. "Want to tell me about Craig's working habits instead?"

"What do you mean?"

"How did he work? There was a sheet of paper in his

138

typewriter on the day he was killed. Did he normally type his stuff?"

"Yes."

"Always? Did he ever write in longhand, for example?"

"Never."

"Did he ever *dictate?*"

"To a secretary, do you mean? No."

"Or into a machine?"

"A recorder?"

"Yes. Did he ever put anything on *tape?*"

The word seemed to resonate in the room. He had not yet told her that Maude Jenkins had typed a portion of Craig's book from a two-hour cassette he'd delivered near the end of the summer three years ago. Hillary did not immediately answer. A log shifted on the grate; the fire crackled and spit.

"Did he?" Carella said.

"Not that I know of."

"What was his voice like?"

"Greg's voice?"

"Yes. I understand he was a heavy smoker. Was his voice hoarse or . . . ?" He searched for another word and finally used the one Maude Jenkins had used in describing the voice on the tape. "Rasping? Would you call it rasping?"

"No."

"At least a portion of *Deadly Shades* was on tape," he said. "About a hundred pages of it. Were there . . . ?"

"How do you know that?"

"I spoke to the woman who typed it. Were there any other tapes? The published book ran something like three hundred pages, didn't it?"

"Close to four hundred."

"So where are the tapes? If the first part of it was on tape . . ."

"I never saw any tapes," Hillary said.

"Who typed the final manuscript?"

"I don't know. I didn't know Greg while he was working on *Shades.*"

"Who *normally* types his stuff? In the city, I mean."

"He hasn't had anything typed recently. He was still working on the new book; he had no reason to have it typed clean till he finished it."

"Would Daniel Corbett have known anything about the existence of any tapes?"

139

"I have no idea," Hillary said, and the candles on the mantelpiece went out.

Carella felt a sudden draft in the room and turned abruptly toward the front door, thinking it might have been blown open by the raging wind. He could see past the edge of the boxed stairwell to the small entryway. The door was closed. He went to it anyway and studied the lock—the same as the one on the kitchen door but securely latched nonetheless. He went out into the kitchen. The hurricane lamps were still burning on the fireplace mantel and the drainboard, but the candles he had lighted on the kitchen table were out—and the kitchen door was open.

He stood looking at the door. He was alone in the room. The extinguished candles sent wisps of trailing smoke up toward the ceiling beams. He put his glass down on the kitchen table, went to the door, and looked at the lock. The thumb bolt had been turned; the spring latch was recessed into the locking mechanism. As earlier, the storm door was closed—but the slip bolt had been thrown back. He heard a sound behind him and whirled instantly. Hillary was standing in the doorway to the kitchen.

"They're here," she whispered.

He did not answer her. He locked both doors again and was turning to relight the candles when the hurricane lamp on the drainboard suddenly leaped into the air and fell to the floor, the chimney shattering, kerosene spilling from the base and bursting into flame. He stamped out the flames, and then felt another draft, and knew without question that something had passed this way.

He would never in his life tell a single soul about what happened next. He would not tell any of the men in the squadroom because he knew they would never again trust a certified lunatic in a shoot-out. He would not tell Teddy because he knew she, too, would never quite trust him completely afterward. He was turning toward where Hillary stood in the doorway when he saw the figure behind her. The figure was a woman. She was wearing a long dress with an apron over it. A sort of granny hat was on her head. Her eyes were mournful; her hands were clasped over her breasts. She would have been frightening in any event, appearing as suddenly as she had, but the terrifying thing about her was that Carella could see through her body and into the small entryway of the house. Hillary turned in the same instant, either sensing the figure behind her or judging it to be there from the look on Carella's face. The woman vanished at once

140

or, rather, seemed swept away by a fierce wind that sucked her shapelessly into the hall and up the stairs to the second floor of the house. A keening moan trailed behind her; the whispered name "John" echoed up the stairwell and then dissipated on the air.

"Let's follow her," Hillary said.

"Listen," Carella said, "I think we should . . ."

"Come," she said, and started up the stairwell.

Carella was in no mood for a confrontation with a restless spirit looking for a John. What did one do when staring down a ghost? He had not held a crucifix in his hands for more years than he cared to remember, and the last time he'd had a clove of garlic around his neck was when he'd had pneumonia as a child and his grandmother had tied one there on a string to ward off the Evil Eye. Besides, were you *supposed* to treat ghosts like vampires, driving stakes into their hearts and returning them to their truly dead states? Did they even *have* hearts? Or livers? Or kidneys? What the hell *was* a ghost? And besides, who believed in them?

Carella did.

He had never been so frightened since the day he'd walked in on a raving lunatic wielding a hatchet, the man's eyes wide, his mouth dripping spittle, someone's severed hand in his own left hand, dripping blood onto the floor as he charged across the room to where Carella stood frozen in his tracks. He had shot the man six times in the chest, finally dropping him an instant before the hatchet would have taken off his nose and part of his face. But how could you shoot a ghost? Carella did not want to go up to the second story of this house. Hillary was already halfway up the stairs, though, and neither did he want to be called chickenshit. *Why not?* he thought. Call *me chickenshit, go ahead. I'm afraid of ghosts. This goddamn house was carried here stick by stick from Salem, where they hanged witches, and I just saw somebody dressed like Rebecca Nurse or Sarah Osborne or Goody Proctor or who-ever the hell, and she was waiting for a man named John, and there ain't nobody here but us chickens, boss.* Adios, he thought, and saw Hillary disappear around the corner at the top of the stairs, and suddenly heard her screaming. He pulled his gun and took the steps up two at a time.

Hillary, courageous ghost hunter that she was, had collapsed in a dead faint on the floor. An eerie blue light bathed the second-story hallway. The hallway was icy cold; it raised the hackles at the back of his neck even before he saw the women standing there. There were four of them. They all were dressed in what looked like late-seventeenth-century garments. He could see through them and beyond them to the window at the end of the hallway where snow lashed the ancient leaded panes. They began advancing toward him. They were grinning. One of them had blood on her hands. And then, suddenly, a sound intruded itself from someplace above—the attic, he guessed. He could not make out the sound at first. It was a steady throbbing sound, like the beat of a muffled heart. The women stopped when they heard the sound. Their heads moved in unison, tilting up toward the beamed ceiling. The sound grew louder, but he still could not identify it. The women shrank from the sound, huddling closer together in the corridor, seeming to melt one into the other, their bodies overlapping and then disappearing entirely, sucked away by the same strong wind that had banished the specter below.

He squinted his eyes against the wind. It died as suddenly as it had started. He stood trembling in the corridor, Hillary on the floor behind him, snowlight piercing the window at the farthest end, the steady throbbing sound above him. No, it was more like a thumping, the slow, steady thump of—

He recognized the sound all at once.

Someone was bouncing a ball in the attic.

He stood just outside the door to the story above, debating whether he should go up there, thinking maybe somebody was working tricks with lights and wind machines, causing apparitions to appear, a theater of the supernatural, designed to cause a psychic to faint dead away and an experienced detective to stand shaking in his sodden loafers. He told himself there couldn't be anything like ghosts—but he had already seen five of them. He told himself there was nothing to fear, but he was terrified. Fanning the air with his pistol, he made his way up the steps to the attic. The stairs creaked under his cautious tread. The ball kept bouncing somewhere above him.

She was standing at the top of the stairs. She was no older than his daughter April, wearing a long gray dress and a faded sunbonnet. She was grinning at him. She was bouncing a ball, and grinning, and chanting in tempo with the bouncing ball. The chant echoed down the stairwell. It took him a moment to realize that she was repeating over and over again the words "Hang them." The ball bounced, and the child grinned, and the words "Hang them, hang them" floated down the stairwell to where he stood with the pistol shaking in his fist. The air around her shimmered; the ball took on an iridescent hue. She took a step down the stairwell, the ball clutched in her fist now. He backed away, and suddenly lost his footing, and went tumbling down the stairs to the floor below. Above him, he heard her laughter. And then, suddenly, the sound of the ball bouncing again.

He got to his feet and turned the pistol up the steps. She was no longer there. On the floor above he could see a blue luminous glow. His elbow hurt where he had landed on it in his fall. He dragged Hillary to her feet, held her limply against him, hefted her painfully into his arms, and went down the steps to the first floor. Above he could still hear the bouncing ball. Outside the house he carried Hillary to where he'd parked the car, the snowflakes covering her clothes till she resembled a shrouded corpse. He heaved her in onto the front seat and then went back to the house—but only to pick up their coats. The ball was still bouncing in the attic.

He heard it when he went outside again, stumbling through the deep snow toward the car. He heard it over the whine of the starter and the sudden roar of the engine. He heard it over the savage wind and the crash of the ocean. And he knew that whenever in the future anything frightened him, whenever any unknown dark terror seized his mind or clutched his heart, he would hear again the sound of that little girl bouncing the ball in the attic—bouncing it, bouncing it, bouncing it.

It was close to ten o'clock when they got back to the hotel. The night clerk handed him a message over the desk. It read: *Calvin Horse called. Wants you to call him at home.* Carella thanked him, accepted the keys to both rooms, and then led Hillary to the elevators. She had been silent from the moment she regained consciousness in the automobile. She did not say a word now on the way up to the second floor. Outside her door, as she unlocked it, she asked, "Are you going straight to bed?"

"Not immediately," he said.

"Would you like a nightcap?"

"I have to make a call first."

"I'll phone room service. What would you like?"

"Irish coffee."

"Good, I'll have one, too. Come in when you're ready," she said, and opened the door and went into the room. He unlocked his own door, took off his coat, sat on the edge of

143

the bed, and dialed Hawes's home number. He debated greeting him as Mr. Horse, but he was in no mood for squadroom humor just now. Hawes picked up on the third ring.

"Hawes," he said.

"Cotton, this is Steve. What's up?"

"Hi, Steve. Just a second, I want to lower the stereo." Carella waited. When Hawes came back on the line, he said, "Where've you been? I called three times."

"Out snooping around," Carella said. He did not mention the ghosts he'd seen; he would *never* mention the ghosts he'd seen. He shuddered involuntarily now at the mere thought of them. "What've you got?"

"For one thing, a lot of wild prints from that pawnshop counter. Some very good ones, according to the lab boys. They've already sent them over to the I.D. Section; we may get a make by morning. I *hope*."

"Good. What else?"

"Our man took another shot at it. This time he tried to hock the gold earrings with the pearls. Place on Culver and Eighth. They're worth close to six hundred bucks, according to Hillary Scott's list."

"What happened?"

"He was prepared this time. Wouldn't show a driver's license, said he didn't drive. The broker would've accepted his Social Security card, but he said he'd left that at home. He produced a postmarked letter addressed to him at Sixteen-twenty-four McGrew. Name on the envelope was James Rader. The broker got suspicious because it looked like the name and address had been erased and then typed over again. He wouldn't have taken it as identification anyway, but it alerted him, you know? So he went in the back room to check our flyer. When he came out again, the guy was gone, and the earrings with him."

"Anything on James Rader?"

"Nothing in the phone directories, I'm running the name through I.D. now. It's most likely a phony. I wouldn't hold my breath. I've also sent the envelope to the lab. There may be prints on it they can compare against the others."

"How about the address?"

"Nonexistent. McGrew runs for six blocks east to west, just this side of the Stem. Highest number on the street is Fourteen-eleven. He pulled it out of thin air, Steve."

"Check for Jack Rawles," Carella said. "The J. R. matches,

144

he may be our man. If there's nothing for him in the city, check the Boston directories for a listing on Commonwealth Avenue. And if there's nothing in those, call the Boston P.D., see if they can come up with a make."

"How do you spell the Rawles?" Hawes asked.

"R-A-W-L-E-S."

"Where'd you get the name?"

"He was renting the house Craig described in his book."

"So what does that mean?"

"Maybe nothing. Check him out. I'll be up for a while yet; give me a ring if you get anything."

"What do you make of all this running around trying to hock the jewels?" Hawes asked.

"Amateur night in Dixie," Carella said. "He needs money, and he doesn't know any fences. What'd he sound like?"

"Who?"

"The guy who tried to pawn that stuff," Carella said impatiently. "James Rader or what*ever* the fuck his name was."

"Steve?" Hawes said. "Something wrong up there?"

"Nothing's wrong. Can you reach those pawnbrokers?"

"Well, they'll be closed now. It's close to . . ."

"Try them at home. Ask them if the guy had a rasping voice."

"A *rasping* voice?"

"A rasping voice, a hoarse voice. Get back to me, Cotton."

He hung up abruptly, rose from the bed, paced the room a moment, and then sat again and dialed Boston Information. In the room next door he could hear Hillary ordering from room service. Carella gave the Boston operator both names—Jack Rawles and James Rader—and asked for a listing on Commonwealth Avenue. She told him she had a listing for a Jack Rawles, but that it was not for Commonwealth Avenue. He wrote down the number anyway and then asked for the address. She told him she was not permitted to give out addresses. He told her testily that he was a police officer investigating a homicide, and she asked him to hold on while she got her supervisor. The supervisor's voice dripped treacle and peanut butter. She explained patiently that it was telephone company policy not to divulge the addresses of subscribers. When Carella explained with equal patience that he was an Isola detective working a homicide case and gave her the precinct number and its address, and the name of his commanding officer, and then his shield number for good measure, the supervisor said, simply and not so patiently, "I'm sorry, sir," and hung up on him.

Angrily he dialed the number the operator had given him for Jack Rawles. In the hallway outside, Carella could hear someone knocking on Hillary's door. He was about to hang up when a woman answered the phone.

"Hello?" she said.

"Mr. Rawles, please," Carella said.

"Sorry, he's out just now."

"Where is he, would you know?"

"Who's this, please?"

"An old friend," he said. "Steve Carella."

"Sorry, Steve, he's out of town," the woman said.

"Who's this?"

"Marcia."

"Marcia, do you know when he'll be back?"

"No, I just got back myself. I'm a flight attendant; I got stuck in London. There's a note here for my boyfriend, says Jack had to go down to the city, won't be back for a couple of days."

"What city?" Carella said.

"*The* city, man," Marcia said. "There's only one city in the entire world, and it ain't Boston, believe me."

"By your boyfriend . . . who do you mean?"

"Jack's roommate, Andy. They've been living together since the fire."

"What fire was that?" Carella said.

"Jack's place on Commonwealth. Lost everything he had in it."

"What's he doing these days?" Carella asked.

"When did you last see him?"

"We met here in Hampstead, three summers ago."

"Oh. Then he's doing the exact same thing. He must've been at the Hampstead Playhouse then, am I right?"

"Still acting?" Carella asked, taking a chance and hoping Jack Rawles hadn't been a stage manager or an electrician or a set designer.

"Still acting," Marcia said. "Or at least *trying* to act. In the summer it's stock. In the winter it's zilch. Jack's always broke, always scrounging for a part someplace. The only time he ever had any money was just before that summer in Hampstead, and he blew it all to rent that house he was staying in. Two thousand bucks, I think it was, for a television commercial he did in the city. I keep telling him he should move down there. What's there for an actor in Boston?"

"I don't remember him mentioning a fire," Carella said, circling back.

"Well, *when* did you say you'd met? Three summers ago? The fire wasn't until . . . let me think."

Carella waited.

"Two years ago, it must've been. Yeah, around this time, two years ago."

"Uh-huh," Carella said. "When did he leave Boston, would you know?"

"The note doesn't say. It had to be sometime after the twentieth, though."

"How do you know?"

"Because *I* left for London on the twentieth, and *Andy* left for California the same day, and *Jack* was still here. Elementary, my dear Watson."

"Where's Andy now?"

"Search me. I just got in a few minutes ago. You want a madhouse during the holidays? Try Heathrow."

"You wouldn't know whether Jack is *still* in the city, would you?"

"Well, if he was back here, I'd know it," Marcia said. "He's the slob of all time. Open the sugar bowl. you're liable to find a pair of his dirty jockey shorts in it."

Carella chuckled and then said, "Does he still have that distinctive speaking voice?"

"Old Bearclaw Rawles, do you mean?"

"Sort of rasping?"

"Like a file," Marcia said.

"You wouldn't know where he's staying in the city, would you?"

"Big city, Steve," she said. "He could be anywhere."

"Yeah," Carella said. "Well, look, tell him I called, okay? Nothing important, just wanted to wish him a Happy New Year."

"Will do," Marcia said, and hung up.

Carella put the receiver back on the cradle. He debated calling Hawes again to tell him he'd made contact and decided against it. If he knew Hawes, he'd be trying the Boston Police right this minute, even *after* he got a telephone number for Rawles. A cup of Irish coffee sounded very good just now. He crossed the room and knocked on the connecting door.

"Come in," Hillary said.

She was sitting dejectedly in an easy chair, the two cups of Irish coffee on a low table before her. She was still wearing the raccoon coat, huddled inside it.

"You okay?" he asked.

"I guess."

He took one of the cups from the table, sipped at it, and licked whipped cream from his lips. "Why don't you drink it before it gets cold?" he said.

She lifted the other cup, but she did not drink from it.

"What's the matter?"

"Nothing."

"Drink your coffee."

She sipped at it, her eyes lowered.

"Want to tell me?"

"No."

"Okay," he said.

"It's just . . . I'm so damn ashamed of myself."

"Why?"

"Fainting like that."

"Well, it *was* pretty scary back there," Carella said, and sat on the edge of the bed.

"I'm *still* scared," Hillary said.

"So am I."

"I don't believe that."

"Believe it."

"My first real manifestation," she said, "and I . . ." She shook her head.

"The first time I faced a man with a gun, I went blind," Carella said.

"Blind?"

"With fear. I saw the gun in his hand, and then I didn't see anything else. Everything went white."

"What happened?" Hillary asked.

"He shot me, and I died."

She smiled and sipped at her coffee.

"What happened was I came to my senses about three seconds before it would have been too late."

"Did you shoot him?"

"Yes."

"Did you kill him?"

"No."

"Have you *ever* killed anyone?"

"Yes."

"Have you ever been shot yourself?"

"Yes."

148

"Why do you keep doing it?"

"Doing what?"

"Police work."

"I like it," he said simply, and shrugged.

"I've been wondering how I can ever . . ." She shook her head again and put down the coffee cup.

"Ever what?"

"Go on doing what I'm doing. After tonight I wonder if I shouldn't simply get a job as a *ribbon* clerk or something."

"You wouldn't be good at it."

"I'm not so good at this either."

"Come on, you're *very* good," he said.

"Sure. Fainting like a . . ."

"I almost didn't come up those stairs after you," Carella said.

"Sure."

"It's the truth. I almost ran out of that damn house."

"Yet you're willing to face men with guns in their hands."

"A gun is a gun. A ghost . . ." He shrugged.

"I suppose I'm glad I saw them," she said.

"So am I."

"I wet my pants, you know."

"No, I didn't know that."

"I did."

"I almost wet mine."

"Fine pair," she said, and smiled again.

The room went silent.

"Do I really look like your wife?" she asked.

"Yes. You know that."

"I'm not sure of anything anymore."

Again the room went silent.

"Well," Carella said, and got to his feet.

"No, don't go yet," she said.

He looked at her.

"Please," she said.

"Well, okay, few minutes," he said, and sat on the edge of the bed again.

"Is your wife anything at all like me?" Hillary asked. "Or is the resemblance purely physical?"

"Purely physical."

"Is she prettier than I am?"

"Well . . . you really look a lot alike."

"I always thought my sister was prettier than I am," Hillary said, and shrugged.

"She thinks so, too."

"She told you that?"

"Yes."

"Bitch," Hillary said, but she was smiling. "Shall we order another round of these?"

"No, I don't think so. We've got a long drive back tomorrow. We'd better get some sleep."

"Yes, we'd better," Hillary said.

"So," he said, and rose again. "I'll leave a call for . . ."

"No, don't go," she said. "I'm still frightened."

"It's really getting late," he said. "We . . ."

"Every time I think of them I shudder."

"There's nothing to be afraid of," he said. "You're here, and our lady friends are miles from . . ."

"Stay with me," she said.

Her eyes met his. He looked into her face.

"Sleep here," she said. "With me."

"Hillary," he said, "thank you, but . . ."

"Just to hold me," she said. "In the night."

"Just to hold you, huh?" he said, and smiled.

"Well, whatever," she said, and returned the smile. "Okay?"

"No," he said. "Not okay."

"I think you'd like to," she said. She was still smiling.

He hesitated. "Yes, I'd like to," he said.

"So what's . . . ?"

"But I won't."

"We're stranded here . . ."

"Yes . . ."

"No one would ever know."

"*I* would know."

"You'd forgive yourself," she said, and her smile widened.

"Hillary, come on, let's quit it, okay?"

"No," she said. "Not okay."

"Look, I . . . come on, really."

"Do you know how my sister would handle this?" she asked. "She'd tell you she washed out her panties the minute she got back here to the room. She'd tell you her panties were hanging on the shower in the bathroom. She'd tell you she wasn't wearing any panties under her skirt. Do you think *that* would interest you?"

"Only if I were in the lingerie business," Carella said, and to his great surprise and enormous relief, Hillary burst out laughing.

"You really *mean* it, don't you?" she said.

"Yeah, what can you do?" Carella said, and shrugged.

"Well, okay then," Hillary said. "I *guess*." She rose, shrugged out of the coat, laughed gently again, murmured, "The *lingerie* business," shook her head, and said, "I'll see you in the morning."

"Good night, Hillary," he said.

"Good night, Steve," she said, and sighed and went into the bathroom.

He stood looking at the closed bathroom door for a moment, and then he went into his own room and locked the door behind him.

He dreamed that night that the door between their rooms opened as mysteriously as the doors at the Loomis house had. He dreamed that Hillary stood in the doorway naked, the light from her own room limning the curves of her young body for an instant before she closed the door again behind her. She stood silently just inside the door, her eyes adjusting to the darkness, and then she came softly and silently to the bed and slipped under the covers beside him. Her hand found him. In the darkness she whispered, "I don't care *what* you think," and her mouth descended.

In the morning, when he awoke, the snow had stopped.

He went to the door between the rooms and tried the knob. The door was locked. But in the bathroom he smelled the lingering scent of her perfume and saw a long black hair curled like a question mark against the white tile of the sink.

He would not tell Teddy about *this* encounter either. Seven ghosts in one night was one more ghost than anybody needed or wanted.

11

The pawnshop stakeout went into effect on December 28, as the result of a squadroom brainstorming session that took place early that morning in Lieutenant Byrnes's office. The lieutenant was sitting behind his desk wearing a blue cardigan sweater—a Christmas gift from his wife, Harriet—over a white dress shirt and a blue tie. His desk was piled with papers. He had told Carella and Hawes that he could give them fifteen minutes of his time, and he looked at the clock now as Carella started his pitch.

"It looks like the man we're after is this Jack Rawles," Carella said. "Came down here from Boston on the day before the murders, wasn't back there yet when I called yesterday."

"Why'd you call?" Byrnes asked.

"Because he rented the house Craig wrote about."

"So?"

"So there're supposed to be ghosts in that house," Carella said, not daring to mention that he had actually *seen* the ghosts who were supposed to be there.

"What's that got to do with the price of fish?" Byrnes said, a favorite expression he never tired of using when his detectives seemed to be making no sense at all.

"I think there's a connection," Carella said.

"What connection?" Byrnes said.

"The typist up there in Hampstead says she typed up a portion of Craig's book from a tape that Rawles may have made."

"How do you know Rawles made it?"

"I don't for sure. But when I talked to his roommate's girl friend, she confirmed that he has a rasping voice. The voice on the tape was described to me as rasping."

"Go ahead," Byrnes said, and looked up at the clock again.

"Okay. Somebody fitting Rawles's description made two attempts to hock two different pieces of jewelry stolen from Craig's apartment on the day of the murder."

"First pawnshop was on Ainsley and Third," Hawes said.

"Second one was on Culver and Eighth. We figure he's holed up somewhere in the precinct and is trying to get rid of the stuff at local pawnshops."

"How many are there in the precinct?" Byrnes asked.

"We get daily transaction reports from seventeen of them."

"Out of the question," Byrnes said at once.

"We wouldn't want to cover all . . ."

"How many then?"

"Eight."

"Where?"

"A ten-block square, north and east from Grover and First."

"Eight shops. That's sixteen men you're asking for."

"Right, sixteen," Carella said.

"Have you checked the hotels and motels for a Jack Rawles?"

"All of them in the precinct. We came up negative."

"How about outside the precinct?"

"Genero's running them down now. It's a long list, Pete. Anyway, we think he's someplace up here. Otherwise, he'd be shopping pawnbrokers elsewhere in the city."

"Where's he staying then? A rooming house?"

"Could be. Or maybe with a friend."

"Sixteen men," Byrnes said again, and shook his head. "I can't spare anybody on the squad. I'd have to ask Frick for uniformed officers."

"Would you do that?"

"I'll need fourteen," Byrnes said.

"Sixteen," Carella said.

"Fourteen plus you and Hawes makes sixteen."

"Yeah, right."

"I wish I could ask him for ten. He's very tight-assed when it comes to assigning his people to special duty."

"We can make do with ten," Carella said, "if you think that'll swing it."

"I'll ask for an even dozen," Byrnes said. "He'll bargain for eight, and we'll settle for ten."

"Good," Carella said. "We'll work up the list of shops we want covered."

"He won't be hitting the two he already tried," Byrnes said. "I'll call the captain. Get your list typed up. When did you want to start?"

"Immediately."

"Okay, let me talk to him."

The stakeout started at ten o'clock that morning, shortly after it began raining. In this city there was a wintertime pattern to the weather. First it snowed. Then it rained. Then it grew bitterly cold, turning the streets and sidewalks to ice. Then it snowed again. And then, more often than not, it rained. And turned to ice again. It had something to do with fronts moving from yon to hither. It was a supreme pain in the ass. Snug in the back room of Silverstein's Pawn Shop on the Stem and North Fifth, Carella and Hawes complained about the weather and sipped hot coffee from soggy cardboard containers. Elsewhere in the precinct, ten uniformed cops were similarly ensconced, waiting for someone fitting Jack Rawles's description to appear, preferably bearing large hunks of jewelry stolen from Craig's apartment.

"There's something I ought to tell you," Hawes said.

"What's that?"

"I took Denise Scott to dinner last night."

"Nothing wrong with that," Carella said.

"Well . . . actually, she was in my apartment when I spoke to you."

"Oh?" Carella said.

"In fact, she was in my bed."

"Oh," Carella said.

"I'm mentioning it only because she'll be a material witness when we get this guy, and I hope that doesn't complicate . . ."

"*If* we get him."

"Oh, we'll get him."

"And *if* he's our man."

"He'll be our man," Hawes said. "He's got to be our man, don't you think?"

"That's what I'm hoping," Carella said.

"Why do you figure he did it?" Hawes asked.

"I'm not sure. But I think . . ." Carella hesitated. Then he said, "I think it was because Craig stole his ghosts."

"Huh?" Hawes said.

Adolf Hitler must have thought of himself as a hero; Richard Nixon probably *still* thinks of himself as one; every man and woman in the world is the hero or heroine of a personal scenario. It was therefore understandable that Carella considered himself the hero in the continuing drama that had started with the murder of Gregory Craig on December 21. He did not for a moment believe that Hawes might similarly consider *himself* the hero. Hawes was his partner.

Heroes sometimes have partners, but they are only there to say, "Kemo sabe." In Hawes's scheme of things, *he* was the hero, and Carella was his partner. Neither of them could possibly have guessed that yet another hero might make the arrest that cracked the case.

Takashi Fujiwara was a twenty-three-year-old patrolman working out of the Eight-Seven. His fellow police officers called him "Tack." Like all men, he considered himself a hero, even more so on this night of December 29, when the stakeout was two days old and the snow had turned again to rain. It was Fujiwara's devout belief that no one in his right mind should be walking a beat in the rain. He wasn't even sure that anyone should be walking a beat at *all*, rain or not. What was the matter with putting all the city's patrolmen in cars? What was all this bullshit about foot patrols deterring crime? Fujiwara had been walking a beat for two years now, and he had not noticed a discernible decline in the city's crime rate. He did not know that at two minutes past five on this shitty, miserable rainy Friday he would become a hero not only in his own mind but in the eyes of his peers. He did not know that before the new year was a week old, he would be promoted to Detective/Third and become an honored and honorable member of the team of men up there on the second floor of the station house. He knew only that he was soaked to the skin.

Fujiwara's parents both had been born in the United States. He was the youngest of four sons and the only one of them to join the police force. His eldest brother was a lawyer in San Francisco. The next two brothers owned a Japanese restaurant downtown on Larimore Street. Fujiwara hated Japanese food, so he rarely visited his brothers in their place of business. His mother kept telling him he should learn to appreciate Japanese cuisine. She kept serving him sashimi. He kept kissing her on the cheek and asking for steak.

It had been his mother's misfortune, when she was just sixteen and when Fujiwara and his three brothers were not even the faintest glimmer in her eye, to accept from her grandmother in Tokyo an invitation to visit her. Reiko Komagome—for such was her maiden name—was at the time attending a private school in the San Fernando Valley, her parents being rather wealthy Japanese immigrants who owned and operated a brisk silk business with its base in Tokyo and its primary American outlet in Los Angeles. Reiko's Thanksgiving holiday started on November 21 that year, and she was not due back at school till December 1. But since her birthday fell on November 10, a Monday, and since a trip to Japan could, after all, be considered an educational and cultural experience, Reiko's mother was able to convince the school authorities to let her out a week and more before the start of the scheduled vacation—provided she diligently did her assigned homework while she was in the Orient. Reiko left for Japan on November 9. Toward the end of her stay there, however, she came down with a severe cold and an attendant fever, and her grandmother was fearful of sending her on the long voyage back to the States. She called Los Angeles and received Reiko's mother's permission to keep her in Tokyo at least until the fever abated.

The year was 1941.

On December 7—when Reiko's temperature was normal and her bags packed—the Japanese bombed Pearl Harbor. She did not return to Los Angeles until the summer of 1946, when she was twenty-one years old. She got married the following year to a man who subsequently taught her the intricacies of the jade business and the joys of sex (Reiko was delighted to learn that Japanese prints did not lie) and who incidentally impregnated her with four handsome sons, the youngest of whom was Tack Fujiwara.

The way Fujiwara got to be a hero and subsequently a Detective/Third came about quite by accident. He had relieved on post at a quarter to five and was walking a singularly dreary stretch of Culver Avenue some three blocks from the station house, an area of grim tenements interspersed with several greasy spoons, a billiard parlor, a check-cashing store, a pawnshop, a bar, and a shop selling tawdry lingerie of the breakaway variety. Most of the stores would be open till six or seven; he would not have to start shaking doorknobs till then. One of the greasy spoons would be open till eleven; the other would close at midnight. The billiard parlor generally closed its doors sometime between 2:00 and 3:00 A.M., depending on how many customers were in there shooting pool. He had checked with the sergeant riding Adam Six, who'd told him to keep his eyes open for a brand-new blue Mercury sedan reported stolen that afternoon and who jokingly advised him not to drown out there in the rain.

At ten minutes to five he stopped by at the billiard parlor to make sure nobody was breaking anybody else's head with a pool cue. At four minutes to five he dropped into the greasy spoon next door and declined the proprietor's proffered cup of coffee, telling him he'd stop back later tonight. He was walking past Martin Levy's pawnshop at precisely two minutes past the hour when the opportunity to become a hero presented itself. The gates on the shop were already up for the night, but a light was still burning inside. Fujiwara saw nothing unusual about this; Mr. Levy often worked inside for a half hour or more after he'd locked up. He did not even glance into the shop. He turned back to look at it only because he heard the bell over the door jingle, and he was surprised to see a hatless dark-haired man running out into the rain with what appeared to be a diamond necklace clutched in his fist.

Fujiwara did not have the faintest inkling that this was Hillary Scott's eighteen-karat gold choker set with diamonds and valued at $16,500. Nor did he know that Levy's shop had been one of those judiciously eliminated from Carella's list because it was impossible to cover eight shops with two men to a shop when there were only an even dozen men available for the job. In fact, Fujiwara didn't even know a stakeout operation was currently in progress at assorted pawnshops in the precinct; such information was rarely passed on to mere patrolmen, lest they behave in ways that might blow the whole undercover scheme. Fujiwara was just a poor wet slob walking his beat and witnessing what looked a hell of a lot like a robbery in progress. As the man ran out of the shop, he stuffed the necklace into the pocket of his coat, and if Fujiwara had entertained any doubts before that moment, they all vanished now. Drawing his pistol, he shouted, "Police officer! Halt, or I'll shoot!" and the fleeing man knocked him flat on his ass on the sidewalk and then trampled over him like a herd of buffalo and continued running for the corner of the block.

Fujiwara rolled over onto his belly and, holding the gun with both hands and propping himself on his elbows the way he'd been taught at the Academy, pulled off two shots in succession at the fleeing man's legs. He missed both times and swore under his breath as the man turned the corner out of sight. Fujiwara was on his feet at once. His gun in his right hand, his black poncho flapping so that he resembled a giant bat flitting through the rain, he reached the corner, and turned it, and found himself face to face with the man he'd been chasing. The man was holding what looked like a bread knife in his right hand.

Not knowing the man was a suspect in three murders, believing only that he'd stolen a piece of jewelry from Mr. Levy's pawnshop, Fujiwara's eyes opened wide in combined fright, surprise, and disbelief. It was one thing to walk into a store where some cheap thief was holding a gun on somebody; in a situation like that you might *expect* an attack. But this guy had already rounded third and was heading for home, so why the hell was he risking a hassle with a cop? *You dope, I'm* a cop! Fujiwara thought, and stepped aside in reflex to dodge the knife. The tip of the knife penetrated the poncho, missing the body by an inch, snagging on the rubberized fabric, and then pulling free again for what Fujiwara hoped would not be a more definitive thrust. This time he didn't bother with the niceties of shooting below the waist. This time he fired straight at the man's chest, and this time he hit him—not in the chest, but in the shoulder, which was plenty good enough. The man reeled back from the force of the slug. The knife dropped from his hand and clattered to the slippery wet pavement. He was turning to run again when Fujiwara said, so softly that it sounded almost like the whisper of the rain, "Mister, you're dead," and the man stopped in his tracks, and nodded his head, and to Fujiwara's great astonishment began weeping.

The formal Q and A took place in Jack Rawles's hospital room at 8:20 P.M. on New Year's Eve. Present were Lieutenant Peter Byrnes, Detective Stephen Louis Carella, Detective Cotton Hawes, and an assistant district attorney named David Saperstein. A police stenographer took down everything that was said. Saperstein asked all the questions; Rawles gave all the answers.

Q: Mr. Rawles, can you tell us when and how you came into possession of the choker you tried to pawn December twenty-ninth?
A: I took it because I was entitled to it.
Q: When was this, Mr. Rawles?
A: I already told the police officers.
Q: Yes, but this is a formal statement you're now making, and I wish you'd repeat it all for me.
A: It was December twenty-first.
Q: How did you come into possession of it on that date?
A: I took it from Gregory Craig's apartment.
Q: Did you steal any other . . . ?
A: I didn't *steal* it. I took it as partial payment of a debt.
Q: What debt?
A: The money Gregory Craig owed me.
Q: How much money did he owe you?
A: Half the receipts on *Deadly Shades*.

158

Q: Deadly shades, did you say?

A: Yes.

Q: Deadly *shades?* I'm sorry, what . . . ?

A: You've got to be kidding.

Q: No, I'm not. What do you mean by deadly shades?

A: It's a book. Gregory Craig was a writer.

Q: Oh, I see. And you took the choker from his apartment because you felt he owed you fifty percent . . .

A: By contract.

Q: You had a contract with Mr. Craig?

A: I did. Fifty percent of the receipts on the book. In black and white and signed by both of us.

Q: I see. And where is that contract now?

A: I don't know. That's why I went up there. To get a copy of it.

Q: We're talking now about December twenty-first, are we?

A: Yes.

Q: Which is when you went to see Mr. Craig to get a copy of the contract.

A: Yes *My* copy got lost in a fire. I used to live on Commonwealth Avenue in Boston. I had a fire in my apartment, the contract went up with everything else.

Q: So . . . if I understand this . . . after the fire, there was only Mr. Craig's copy of the contract.

A: Yes. Which is why I went up there. To see if I could get it.

Q: What time did you get there, Mr. Rawles?

A: At about five o'clock.

Q: We are referring now to Seven-eighty-one Jackson Avenue, are we?

A: Yes. Craig's apartment.

Q: And you got there at five o'clock on the evening of December twenty-first.

A: Yes.

Q: What did you do when you got there?

A: I told the security guard I was Daniel Corbett. I knew Corbett had been the editor on the book. I read a story about them in *People* magazine.

Q: Why did you use a false name?

A: Because I knew Craig wouldn't let me up otherwise. I'd written letters to him; I'd tried calling him. He never answered my letters, and he used to hang up when I called. Finally, he changed his phone number. That's why I came down to the city. To talk to him personally. To demand my share of the money.

Q: What happened when you went upstairs?

A: I rang the doorbell, and Craig looked out at me through the peephole. I told him I didn't want any trouble; I just wanted to talk to him.

Q: Did he open the door for you?

A: Yes, but only because I told him I was going to go see the district attorney if he wouldn't talk to me.

Q: We are referring now to Apartment Three-oh-four, are we?

A: Yes, I guess so. I don't remember what apartment it was. The security guard told me, and I went up, but I don't remember now what the number was.

Q: What happened after you entered the apartment?

A: We sat down and talked.

Q: What about?

A: The money he owed me. He knew I'd had that fire; I was stupid enough to write to him afterward and ask him for a copy of the contract.

Q: You talked about the money . . .

A: Yes. By my calculations, he owed me something like eight hundred thousand dollars. I was supposed to get half of everything, you see. The royalties on the hardcover edition alone came to something like four hundred thousand dollars. The paperback rights sold for a million and a half, and the author's share of that was seven hundred and fifty thousand. His publishers got ten percent on the movie sale but that still left him with four hundred fifty thousand. You add that up, it comes to a million six, and half of that is eight hundred thousand. He never gave me a nickel.

Q: Did you ask him for the money?

A: When do you mean?

Q: When you were there talking with him.

A: Of *course* I asked him for the money. That's why I was there. To *demand* the money. To tell him that if he didn't pay me every cent, I would go to the district attorney.

Q: What was his reaction to that?

A: He told me to sit down and relax. He asked me if I'd like a drink.

Q: Did you accept a drink?

A: I did.

Q: Did *he* have a drink, too?

A: He had two or three of them.

Q: And you?

A: The same. Two or three.

Q: What happened then?

A: He told me I could go to the district attorney if I liked, but it wouldn't do me any good. My copy of the contract had been lost in the fire, and he'd destroyed *his* copy, so now there was no record of the transaction. He said I didn't have a leg to stand on. He said if I felt I had any cause for legal action, I should go to his publishers instead, and they'd laugh in my face. Those were his exact words. Laugh in my face.

Q: Why *hadn't* you gone to his publishers before then?

A: Because I knew he was right. I didn't have the contract; I didn't even have the tapes. Why would they have believed me?

Q: What tapes are you referring to, Mr. Rawles?

A: I put it all down on tape for him. All my experiences in the house up there in Hampstead. We got to talking about it one day in a bar, and he said he found it all very interesting, and told me he was a writer, and then asked if I'd put it all on tape for him. We taped it in the house he was renting that summer—but only after he'd proposed his deal. Fifty-fifty. He'd get the book sold, and he'd give me fifty percent of what it earned. I told him no; I wanted my name on the book, too; I wanted to share the by-line. I figured that would help me. I'm an actor. I figured my name on the book would help me get parts later on.

Q: Did he agree to putting your name on the book?

A: No. He told me he would never be able to sell it with a split by-line on it. So I said okay. I figured fifty percent of the profits would carry me a long way.

Q: And this is what was in the contract?

A: Yes, in black and white. He wrote the contract himself, and we both signed it. A simple letter agreement, but binding.

Q: Did an attorney check it for you?

A: No, I couldn't afford an attorney. I'm an actor.

Q: All right, Mr. Rawles, on the evening of December twenty-first, sometime after five o'clock while you and Mr. Craig were drinking together—

A: Yes.

Q: —he told you that going to the district attorney would do you no good.

A: That's right.

Q: What happened then?
A: I took out the knife.
Q: What knife?
A: A knife.
Q: Yes *what* knife?
A: I had it in my dispatch case. I brought it down from Boston.
Q: Why?
A: Just in case.
Q: Just in case of what?
A: In case I had to scare him or anything. This man hadn't answered any of my letters; he used to hang up the phone. I thought maybe I'd have to scare him into giving me my share of the money.
Q: And is that why you took the knife out of the dispatch case? To scare him?
A: Yes.
Q: What happened then?
A: I forced him into the bedroom.
Q: And then?
A: He tried to get the knife from me.
Q: Yes?
A: So I stabbed him.
Q: You killed him because he tried to . . .
A: No, he wasn't dead. I rolled him over and tied his hands behind him with a coat hanger. Then I began searching the place. I believed what he'd said about having destroyed his copy of the contract, but I thought maybe he still had the tapes hidden someplace in the apartment. The tapes with my voice on them. The tapes with *me* telling the story. They would have been *proof*, you see. So I began looking for them.
Q: Did you find them?
A: No.
Q: What did you do then?
A: I stabbed him again.
Q: Why?
A: Because I was angry. He'd stolen my story, and he hadn't paid me for it.
Q: Was he dead when you left the apartment?
A: I didn't know if he was dead or not. When I read the paper later, it said he'd been killed.
Q: The Coroner's report states that Mr. Craig was stabbed nineteen times.
A: I don't know how many times I stabbed him. I was angry.

162

Q: But you didn't know he was dead. You stabbed him nineteen times—

A: I told you I don't know how many times.

Q: —yet you didn't know he was dead.

A: That's right, I didn't.

Q: What'd you do then?

A: I took everything I could find. As partial payment of the debt. And then I washed the glasses we'd been drinking from, and I left the apartment.

Q: Why'd you wash the glasses?

A: Fingerprints. Don't you think I know about fingerprints? Everybody knows about fingerprints.

Q: What happened when you left the apartment?

A: A woman saw me. I got through the lobby okay, but then this woman saw me on the street. I had blood on my clothes, I was running from the building, and she looked at me funny. I had the knife under my coat. I . . . I just took it out and stabbed her.

Q: Was this Marian Esposito?

A: I didn't know who she was at the time.

Q: When did you learn who she was?

A: There was something in the newspaper. I figured it had to be her.

Q: Mr. Rawles, did you kill Daniel Corbett?

A: Yes.

Q: Why?

A: Because afterwards . . . you see, afterwards when I began thinking about it . . . well, I knew Corbett was his editor, and I'd given *his* name to the security guard, so I thought . . . what I thought was maybe there was some chance Corbett had heard the tapes. Maybe there was a possibility he *knew* this was really *my* story. And if that was the case, then maybe he'd tell the police about me, tell them Jack Rawles had a . . . well . . . a grudge against Craig and they'd come looking for me. So I went to see him.

Q: With the object of killing him?

A: Well . . . just to make sure.

Q: Make sure of what?

A: That he wouldn't tell anyone about a possible connection between me and Craig. I had a hard time finding him. He isn't listed in the telephone book; I didn't know where he lived. So finally, I went to Harlow House and waited for him to come out after work . . .

Q: How did you know what he looked like?

163

A: There was a picture of him and Craig in *People* magazine. I knew what he looked like. I followed him home, and then I . . . I guess I killed him.

Q: And did you also try to kill Denise Scott?

A: I don't know anyone named Denise Scott.

Q: Hillary Scott?

A: Hillary, yes.

Q: You tried to kill her?

A: Yes.

Q: Why?

A: For the same reason. I thought Craig might have mentioned me to her. I knew they were living together; she answered the phone sometimes when I called. I followed her from the apartment the day after I . . . the day after I killed Craig. She was there with these two police officers, I saw them coming out of the apartment together. She had another apartment in Stewart City, the name Scott was on the mailbox. I thought she might be dangerous, you see. I didn't want anyone else to know about me. There was someone else who . . .

Q: Yes?

A: No, never mind.

Q: What were you about to say?

A: Only that someone else knew.

Q: Who was that?

A: Stephanie Craig. His ex.

Q: Mr. Craig's former wife?

A: Yes.

Q: Knew what?

A: About the tapes. She heard the tapes one day. We were sitting there in his living room, playing them back, when she came to see him. The machine was going; she heard them.

Q: Why had she come to see him?

A: She was always stopping by. She was still carrying the torch for him.

Q: And she heard the tapes?

A: Yes. But I didn't have to worry about her, you see. She drowned that very same summer.

All the way uptown from Buena Vista Hospital to Mercy General, where Meyer Meyer was recuperating, Carella thought about Jack Rawles's statement. The motives for murder would never cease to amaze him, but discounting the

164

murder of Marian Esposito—which, as he'd suspected from the start, was a murder of expedience—the motives for the killings of Gregory Craig and Daniel Corbett were complex and contradictory. Rawles had gone to see Craig because he wanted recognition, by way of payment, for his contribution to a phenomenal best-seller. He had slain Craig because recognition had been denied him. And then he had killed Corbett and tried to kill Hillary because he had been afraid of the very thing he'd so desperately wanted earlier: recognition.

There were holes in the statement; there were always holes. Not anything that would prevent a conviction, no. Saperstein had done a good job nailing down all the facts, and Carella suspected the D.A.'s Office would have no trouble convincing a jury that Jack Rawles had indeed killed three people during the holiday season and tried to kill a fourth. But as he parked the car in the lot outside Mercy General, and as he took the elevator up to Meyer's room on the sixth floor, he wondered about that odd collaboration three summers ago and wondered how Craig had finally convinced Rawles to surrender the one true recognition he should have insisted on: his name on the book. In many respects, Rawles was exactly what Hillary had labeled him, a ghost—in literary terms, at least. He had, in effect, already written the book for Craig the day he taped his experiences. And he had been denied the one thing that might have given him something more than cetoplasmic substance—a shared by-line.

Carella wondered, too—and this bothered the hell out of him—about the drowning of Stephanie Craig. She had heard Rawles's voice on those tapes, she undoubtedly knew that Craig was writing a book, and if psychics were to be believed, she had threatened to reveal that the material was stolen, that Craig's book was not really his own but instead another man's. But had she *truly* threatened Craig with exposure, or was that only a figment of Hillary Scott's vivid psychic imagination? Because if she *had* threatened him and if Craig *was* indeed responsible for her drowning, then he had begun planning the theft away back then when the book was still in progress, with no intention of *ever* honoring his contract with Rawles.

Sighing, Carella went down the corridor to Meyer's room.

Meyer was sitting up in bed, reading. He put the book aside the moment Carella came into the room, and extended his hand, and listened while Carella told him first about how the case had been wrapped by a patrolman named Tack Fujiwara and then about Rawles's statement and the questions it had left unresolved.

"It bothers me that I don't have all the answers," Carella said.

"Listen," Meyer said, "if you had all the answers, you'd be God."

Carella smiled. Meyer returned the smile. The two men shook hands again and wished each other a happy new year, and then Carella went home to Riverhead. Fanny had already left for her sister's home in Calm's Point. They allowed the twins to stay up till midnight and even permitted them to have a sip of champagne when they toasted the new year. Later, after they had put the children to sleep, they made love, a tradition they had honored since the first year of their marriage because—as Teddy put it—she believed in starting each new year with a bang.

In the middle of the night Carella woke up and sat staring into the room, still troubled by the realization that he would *never* know for sure whether Gregory Craig had killed his former wife. And then he went back to sleep because he *wasn't* God after all, and maybe in the greater scheme of things there were answers he never dreamed of.

ABOUT THE AUTHOR

ED MCBAIN is Evan Hunter, but millions know him as Ed McBain, the top cop writer in the world and author of the 87th Precinct books. Praised by *The New York Times* as "the best of today's procedural school of police stories," the series now has over 53,000,000 copies in print around the world. McBain has been writing the 87th Precinct thrillers for the past twenty-three years. Fans can count on the realism of police activities in the series for, as the author explains, "I had to research very carefully by riding squad cars, attending police line-ups and visiting labs." Thus, the details are authentic and have become a McBain trademark.

McBain, a.k.a. Evan Hunter, grew up on the tough city streets of New York with one main ambition: to get out. At first he thought his ticket out would be his artistic skills, but during a two-year stint in the Navy, he discovered a new talent: writing short stories. When he returned two years later, he attended Hunter College, then spent a disastrous few months teaching high school. Hunter turned that experience into a sizzling novel, later made into a film, called *Blackboard Jungle*. He's been writing steadily since that time (as Ed McBain with the 87th Precinct series) and the Evan Hunter novel, *The Chisholms*, was a CBS mini-series. He's also written *Strangers When We Meet*, *Last Summer* and the script for Hitchcock's celebrated horror film, *The Birds*.

Ross Macdonald
Lew Archer Novels

"The finest series of detective novels ever written by an American . . . I have been reading him for years and he has yet to disappoint. Classify him how you will, he is one of the best novelists now operating, and all he does is keep on getting better."

—The New York Times

☐	13963	FIND A VICTIM	$2.25
☐	13235	THE GALTON CASE	$2.25
☐	12926	THE MOVING TARGET	$1.95
☐	12914	FAR SIDE OF THE DOLLAR	$1.95
☐	12337	THE NAME IS ARCHER	$1.95
☐	12115	SLEEPING BEAUTY	$2.25
☐	13789	THE BLUE HAMMER	$2.25

Buy them at your local bookstore or use this handy coupon for ordering:

WHODUNIT?

Bantam did! By bringing you these masterful tales of murder, suspense and mystery!

Bantam Book Catalog

Here's your up-to-the-minute listing of over 1,400 titles by your favorite authors.

This illustrated, large format catalog gives a description of each title. For your convenience, it is divided into categories in fiction and non-fiction—gothics, science fiction, westerns, mysteries, cookbooks, mysticism and occult, biographies, history, family living, health, psychology, art.

So don't delay—take advantage of this special opportunity to increase your reading pleasure.

Just send us your name and address and 50¢ (to help defray postage and handling costs).

BANTAM BOOKS, INC.
Dept. FC, 414 East Golf Road, Des Plaines, Ill. 60016

Mr./Mrs./Miss_____
(please print)

Address_____

City_____State_____Zip_____

Do you know someone who enjoys books? Just give us their names and addresses and we'll send them a catalog too!

_____

Mr./Mrs./Miss_____

Address_____

City_____State_____Zip_____

Mr./Mrs./Miss_____

Address_____

City_____State_____Zip_____

FC—9/76